TORN BETWEEN TWO BROTHERS

BOX SET

INCLUDES
VOLUMES I, II, III

(2014 Print Edition)

by

Monique Farrow

Cover Design by: Dzine18

Published by: E-Ink It

TORN BETWEEN TWO BROTHERS

VOLUME I

Chapter One

Nothing got me wetter than fantasizing about getting pregnant. You could call me old fashioned, crazy, or just plain dumb. But it was all I thought about. In fact, my boo Darius was plunging deep inside my kitty from behind, while I cheered on his handsome swimmers in my mind. His massive hands wrapped around my tiny waist as he rhythmically beat it up. The shit was feeling so good, I purred in pleasure while teething his white Egyptian sheets. Greedily I threw my ass back, determined to take every inch of his manhood. I could feel my baby speeding up as I crossed my fingers, and hoped his players scored a goal. Darius slapped my ass, and the sound reverberated in his decked out master bedroom.

Turning around, I moaned, "I love you."

"I love you too." He grunted, before pulling out, and exploding onto my back.

"What the fuck, Darius! We're trying to get pregnant remember?" I jumped out of bed with a scowl on my face. Crossing my arms, I gave him the evil eye.

"Aw Fatty, I'm sorry. I forgot." He said, falling onto his back, satisfied and exhausted.

Standing over him, I seriously considered popping the shit out of him. But then, I surveyed his honey brown skin, ripped body, and super cute dimples, and changed my mind. Besides, we'd been together for over four years. Maybe it wasn't a long time to some, but it was more than long enough for me, because I desperately wanted a baby with him. For years, I wasted my time working at build a nigga work shop. Thank god, I resigned from that position, a long time ago. Finally I found a real man with ambition and drive. His money was good, his house was laid, and doors opened up where ever he went. He was definitely the type of man I wanted raising my children. I'd seen him carry the weight of the world on his shoulders without flinching. So I knew he could handle me and a baby, without a problem.

Darius was my personal genie. He gave me everything I ever asked for, except for what I really wanted. A ring and a baby. The ring, I could do without. Correction. Of course, I wanted a rock eventually. But for now, we could go down to the justice of the peace, and file some paper work. I wasn't picky. The baby on the other hand, I wanted asap. How could he forget, the most important thing to me. I'd been buying baby clothes, toys, and booties for over six months. I even had an entire room dedicated to baby at my place.

"Fatty. I forgot." He said, breaking my thoughts.

"Did you Darius? I thought we talked about this."

"We did. We're on the same page baby. I just forgot, damn. You forgive me?" He said, sitting on the edge of the bed in front of me, wearing the cutest pout I've ever seen.

"I guess. And one more thing. I told you, my name is Fatima, stop calling me Fatty. I don't like it."

"I don't like it. He mimicked, while scooping me up in his arms.

"What do you care, girl? You need some fat on your bones anyway. You're so tall and skinny."

"Skinny? Who you calling skinny." I played, punching him in the chest.

"If it wasn't for your tits and ass, you wouldn't have no meat on your bones."

"Good. That's exactly how I like it." I replied, mushing him with a pillow.

I got out of bed, tied my long coily hair in a bun, and grabbed my overnight bag, before heading towards the shower.

"You gonna join me." I asked, before leaving the room.

"In a minute. I gotta make a phone call." He looked a bit stressed which was unusual. Sex

3

usually cleared his mind. We'd have to go another round in the shower. I didn't want him walking around uptight. It couldn't be healthy for his sperm. I wanted a relaxed happy baby, not a tiny tyrant.

"Don't be too long." I said, raising my brows.

"You serious? You know, I'm right behind you."

"You better be." I said, swaying my hips as I walked out the room. I didn't bother glancing over my shoulder to see if he was still watching. I knew he was. Darius couldn't help ogling my goodies.

Hot water fell onto my naked body as I thought about our relationship. Darius had been acting strange recently, and I couldn't figure out why. Last night, we went clubbing with my girl Tasha, and what I like to call her d.o.n, or dick on the night, and Darius hardly said anything. He didn't drink, laugh, or dance, and he always got turned up. Usually, I'm the sole designated driver, because I have a class of rowdy third graders to teach Monday through Friday. Last night was different. He was sipping ginger ale with me.

I tried to ignore the nagging voice in the back of my head saying he didn't want to start a family. I thought my dream of losing my virginity to the same man I'd raise a family with and marry was about to come true, but it seemed like he was getting cold feet. I planned to move in with him, after he committed to me by giving me a ring or baby. I preferred to get married first, but in reality no commitment could be stronger than a blood bond. We would always share a child. Even if, we didn't share a last name. Recently, he'd been pressuring me to move in, but I refused every time. I knew he loved me more than any other woman he'd ever been with in the past, because he told me so. But even the most patient man wouldn't wait forever. Maybe, he'd been acting strange, because I wouldn't move in yet.

"What was that?" I think I heard something. Turning off the water, I stuck my head out the shower door, and froze. I wasn't tripping. Whatever it was, I heard it again. I jumped out the shower, and put on my white cotton robe, before jetting down the staircase.

"Fuck that nigga." Darius yelled into his cell phone.

Downstairs was a mess. Every photo on the wall was crooked, or on the floor. A remote was sticking out the middle of the television screen hanging on the wall. His expensive leather couches were flipped on their backs. It looked like a cyclone ran through the middle of the living room.

"Baby what's going on."

Darius flipped his hand at me, and continued to talk. "How the fuck did he get caught? It was your responsibility to keep shit in line. Now, my ass is

5

blowing in the wind."

Darius was acting like the Tasmanian Devil. He was throwing statues, books, and lamps. Practically, any and everything in his path was tossed across the room. I was stuck. I watched him destroy the house, silently. I'd seen him upset before, but never angry, and especially not psychotically enraged like this.

"250 grand! Nigga are you crazy? I don't have that kinda money. Who the fuck does this fool think he is? You better fix this shit."

Darius hurled his cell phone through the floor length window lining the entry way. He balled up his hands, and started pacing the floor, before slamming his fist against the masonry fireplace. Blood spilled from his knuckles, and down the length of his arms, but he kept at it.

"Baby what are you doing? Stop it! You're hurting yourself." I pleaded, running to his aid.

He ignored me, and continued to grunt and howl. It was like he was lost in a trance. I felt ghostly. He seemed blind, and deaf to everything I did. I grabbed his back, and attempted to pull him away. His elbow knocked me square in the nose, sending me careening back onto the floor.

"Oh shit! I'm sorry, baby. I'm sorry." He said, running to me on the floor.

6

Darius ripped his shirt in half. Then, he tore off a corner piece, and used it to stop my nose bleed. He rocked me in his arms, and kept telling me how sorry he was. Apparently, I needed to get hurt in order for him to hear me.

"Honey, its okay. What's going on?" I asked, concerned.

Sitting in front of me, he clasped both of my hands, and stared straight into my eyes. "I may have to serve some time." He said in one breath.

"You're going to prison?" I was horrified. I couldn't have heard him correctly. "What the hell are you talking about?"

He tightened his grip on my hands, and shook his head. He was irritated, but I was scared. I didn't know where all this was coming from. I tried to pull my hands from him, to wipe away the tears, but he wouldn't let me. It was like holding onto me gave him strength. "Babe. Just listen to me for a minute, damn. It's hard enough saying this shit, once. I won't repeat it, again."

I didn't disobey him. I never did. I just nodded, as tears streamed down my face. I was ready to listen.

"I think, I'm caught up. Eddie, my leg man, got snatched. The feds are putting steaks in front of him, trying to get him to eat. But according to my

7

man, Tool, Eddie ain't biting, yet anyway. They're trying to get me for some work I put in last year. I can't go into the details. Just trust, I'm facing some serious time. According to Tool, Eddie will take the wrap. If, I keep him comfortable while he's serving time, down south. He wants 250 G's before his hearing date, which is about 90 days from now. Babe, I can't get locked up. And you know, I ain't got that kinda of money laying around. I spent all my reserves paying my lawyer for the last case, they were trying to pin on me."

I never saw Darius so scared in my life. He always had a plan A,B, and C. Now that I think about it, he was so good at what he did, I never heard about any business problems, until now.

"I've been trying to go legit. But nobody wants to give a nigga a chance. They want to check my work history, credit score, educational background, and some more shit. How the fuck, am I supposed to change my life around, if nobody will call me back to interview, let alone hire me?"

As I listened to Darius talk, I started thinking about the beginning of our relationship. I was so captivated by him. It didn't take long before I was handing over my V card. I met him during my freshman year at the University of Central Oklahoma. I was eighteen, and naive. He claimed to be in law school. I didn't question a word he said, because he oozed success from his nice clothes down to his sleek ride.

Eventually he told me, he was an entrepreneur into alternative business like the Italians. He wasn't hurting anybody like hustlers on the street slinging rock, running hoes, or knocking over banks. His business was different. He liked to say, he borrowed financial information from people who didn't need it anymore. He simply used social security numbers from dead and old people to finance a better life for himself. He constantly told me, he only committed victimless crimes, which technically didn't make it a crime at all. No one ever got hurt. But right about now, I felt like a victim, because my baby could be leaving me soon.

I was kicking myself for being so naive. I told him, I didn't want to know anything about what he did. As a result, I didn't have to deal with my conscious, and he didn't have to talk about his business. Up until today, the arrangement worked perfectly for both of us. Even when my girl, Tasha told me he was feared on the street. I didn't believe her, that's how much I was in denial. Darius was so syrupy sweet to me, and everyone I'd ever seen him around, I couldn't imagine him hurting a fly. Today, I saw the man she was talking about. I didn't know he was capable of getting so angry.

"Fatima. Are you even listening to me?" His irritated voice, snapped me out of my thoughts.

"Yes, D. I just don't know what to say. We were finally going to start our family. I'm just disappointed."

He was looking at me like I had shit on my face. "That's what you have to say to me, after all that?" He threw my hands, and stood up.

"Baby, wait don't be like that." I got up, and tried to comfort him.

"I'm worried about losing my freedom. Meanwhile, you're still on this baby shit. What the fuck is wrong with you? You think we should have a baby? Even in this situation? I'm starting to think you love my nut, more than me. Fuck you, the baby, and our engagement."

What he said hit me like daggers in the chest. "Darius. That came out wrong. I'm worried about you too, baby. I just thought we'd finally be happy. I can't help feeling a little disappointed."

"We'd finally be happy, or you, Fatima? Because, you're the only that's been pushing this shit, not me."

"What about us being on the same page. All that was bullshit, you said to me a minute ago?"

"No. That wasn't bullshit. This conversation is some bullshit. Matter-of-fact, I think you should leave?"

"Darius?" I pleaded.

10

He didn't respond. He just looked straight through me.

"You seriously want me to go?" I crossed my arms, and waited. "You're just going to kick me out your house, then?"

"Did I stutter? He said, staring me down.

I couldn't believe how hostile he was being. I looked around at the broken glass, trash, and leaning pictures on the wall, and realized it was probably for the best. I headed upstairs to get my bag, and accidentally found my reflection in the bathroom mirror. I looked terrible. My hair was a mess sitting on top of my head. Plus, I had dried blood hanging out my nose. The conversation downstairs was so heavy and dark, I completely forgot about my noise and the pain. He definitely was tripping.

I jogged downstairs ready to go, and saw Darius sitting on the couch with his head in his hands. He studied me, but didn't say anything. Obviously, there was something he wanted to say. So I stood at the bottom of the stairs and waited.

"I don't know what to say. So, I'm just going to say, see you later." He said, getting up to leave.

"Yeah. Whatever." I brushed past him, and through the front door.

Exhausted, I didn't want to say anything to stir

up a new conversation. We'd been together for years, and he never spoke to me the way he did today. I could actually say I was happy to leave. Thank god, I didn't get rid of my apartment. We had petty disagreements that were uncomfortable at worse, but never a true heated argument. Bickering and fighting has never been my style, I try to keep the peace. If our first fight was any indication of what was to come. I definitely wouldn't be sticking around for much longer. I'd leave his ass alone, first.

I jumped into my black 2008 Toyota Camry and backed out of his driveway. Funny, I remembered pulling into his house, hoping to have a little Darius, soon. Now, I didn't know where our relationship was headed, or what I'd gotten myself into.

Chapter Two

Tasha shot up, and the chair went flying behind her. "Girl, no that nigga didn't. He put his hands on you? Let me get my glock." She reached for an invisible gun in her coochie cut shorts. Then, she sat back down at the dining room table, shaking her head.

I sucked my teeth, and rolled my eyes. I was kicking myself for telling her crazy ass what happened. I loved Tasha. She was my girl, and the closest thing I had to family. But she simply did too damn much. Her ass didn't have a sling shot, let alone a gun. Her tiny apartment was cute, but it was no stage. Even though, she was putting on shows. I could picture her saying, "lights, camera, action" before her Oscar worthy performances, every time.

We met years ago, working at a local fast food joint. She was sixteen years old, and weeks away from having her second daughter, Nikki. Her mom stayed firm, and kicked her out after discovering she was pregnant again. She didn't want to help raise, Octavia, Tasha's oldest daughter let alone another child. Their relationship was, and still is awful. Me and Tasha were inseparable, because we both understood the struggle. I was awol from a girl's home, because living in the system became too much. At the time, we were both struggling to get our own place which was a bitch. We've been family ever since.

"Girl, it couldn't have been me. I would have capped his ass." She said, snapping me out of my thoughts.

"Tasha, sit your butt down. And listen. The man didn't hit me. I told you, I ran into his elbow."

"Child boo" She said, waving her hand in my direction. "Don't we all, honey? I saw the same episode of Lucy, child. Next time, you'll be saying the door knob blacked your eye. I told you to get rid of that thirsty ass nigga. If a man seems to good to be true, it's because, he is."

My girl, had it out for Darius. On second thought, Tasha had it out for anyone with a penis. Of course, this time she had a valid reason to give him the side eye, but never before. You'd think she'd appreciate the gifts we give the kids. These bums out here, had my girl jaded. She thought every man was no good. She actually took pride in hustling them out of their money. A fair exchange was no robbery, according to her.

Tiny feet came pitter-pattering into the dining room. Nikki was so excited to talk, she knocked over Tasha's solo cup of gin, and my cup of apple juice. Tasha could definitely handle her liquor, unlike me. I couldn't even tell she'd been drinking.

"Damn. Nikki. Watch where you're going."

"Sorry Mama."

"What is it girl?"

"Tavia hit Daddy right in his eyeball." She said, pretending to get hit herself in the face.

I couldn't help laughing. The child certainly had her mother's flair for drama. As if on cue, DeMarcus came walking into the kitchen holding his eye with dried streams stuck on his face. He was the youngest of Tasha's three kids. They were all stair steps. Octavia was seven, Nikki was six, and DeMarcus was four years old.

"Girl hold on a minute."

I already knew what was coming next. She went into the back room with a fly swatter. Tasha definitely didn't believe in sparing the rod, or spoiling the child. I could hear Octavia crying out in pain as Tasha lashed her for hitting her little brother. My heart silently cried with her. Her aching voice reminded me of all the times, I was beaten as a child. Growing up in the system wasn't easy. In fact, it was a living nightmare. Sometimes, I didn't think I would make it till eighteen. I regularly thought about taking myself. Believing no one would miss me anyway. I took a moment to thank god for bringing Darius and Tasha into my life. Even though, I disagreed with her parenting, I knew better than to tell a parent how to raise their child. That was one of the first lessons I learned as a new teacher, this year.

DeMarcus climbed up on my lap, and instantly sweetened my thoughts. I just wanted to eat him up. Damn, I wanted a child so bad. He gazed up at me with his big doe eyes, and I swear, I almost melted off the chair.

"Hi Aunty Fatty," he said, rubbing his eye, and laying his head against my chest." My eyes stung when he called me Fatty, I couldn't help thinking about my boo. What would I do, if he got locked up? He'd been my life for the last four years. I prayed he was okay.

"Boy get down." Tasha said, shooing him away with the fly swatter.

"That boy is always in your face."

"Don't be messing with my baby. You know me and Darius, love having him over." I said, laughing and kissing him in his dimpled cheek. Tasha didn't like me bringing him to Darius's house. But I insisted he needed a male remodel, and she couldn't disagree. DeMarcus jumped down, and ran into the back room, while Tasha made herself comfortable at the table again.

Looking across the table, I thought about how hard my friend's life must be. She was only nineteen years old, and on her third child, which is why I regularly took the kids. I liked taking the stress off her shoulders every once and awhile. I knew she needed a break every once, and awhile. I especially enjoyed watching little man. He was the closest thing I had to a baby. Besides, Darius liked seeing me in my element because, he didn't have to hear about me wanting a baby. When I was content taking care of DeMarcus. I smiled thinking about our little play dates.

"I know. I know. He's so cute. And all that shit. You can take his ass, if you want. Anyway, lets get back to the tea. So, he busted your nose, and then what happen." She said, peering at me from across the table. Sometimes, I couldn't stand her butt.

I picked up my juice, and rolled my eyes at her high yellow ass, before going on with the story.

"Anyway, he ran into some really bad business problems, that sent him over the edge. The argument wasn't even about us or having a baby. He's emotions just got the best of him."

I love my girl Tasha, but I can't put his business out in the street. I wasn't about to tell her butt, everything, in case he was able to feed the bird, in order to stay out of jail. All she needed to know is that he didn't want to have a baby anymore.

"I knew he was one of those Wall Street types. Money ain't everything child. If he loses his

17

business, what's he going to do, girl? Throw himself out the window." She said, cackling.

"Its not about the business, my nose, or money. I want to have a baby. And now he's saying he doesn't want to. In fact, he said he didn't want to get married either."

"What's your problem girl? You know he was just talking out of his ass. He still loves you. Have some faith. Besides, kids aren't that great, believe me. You're 22 years old, you have plenty of time for babies. Enjoy yourself. Shit, you can take one, or all of mine. I'll even give you a discount. Take one, get the other pair free. While supplies last." She said, half joking. We both cracked up.

I couldn't help feeling a little pissed off. How was she going to be such a hypocrite. She had three people to love. I just wanted one little person to call my own. If she wasn't my sister, I'd check her ass. She knew, how sensitive I was about this topic. I thought, she'd understand. It felt like I was the only member on Team Baby.

Chapter Three

My kids really tried me today. They were so bad. I stopped and wondered, why I even decided to become a teacher. I must have lost my mind. The muscles in the back of my neck tightened, and my head screamed for Tylenol, as I drove home after a long day's work. All I could do was imagine myself falling into my California king sized bed, with a remote in hand, prepared to watch a few hours of ratchet reality television in order to release some stress. I hadn't checked in on Joseline, Stevie J, and Mimi in awhile. They always seemed to be a good distraction, which I desperately needed, after the last few days.

Pulling into my reserved parking space, I looked up, and my heart almost leaped out my chest. The lights were on inside my apartment. How the hell was that possible? Did I forget to turn them off? Maybe, I did. No. That's impossible. I remembered turning them off before leaving for work in the morning. In fact, I double checked.

Cutting off my car engine, I sat and thought about what to do. I'd watched one too many episodes of the First 48 to go upstairs unarmed, and ill prepared. I opened my glove compartment and stared at the little handgun, Darius gave me. He told me to carry it around just in case, some fool wanted to try something stupid, but I never touched the thing. I never dreamed, I would have to use it. I couldn't help wracking my brain with possible scenarios. Who could be up there? Maintenance, maybe? I knew, I didn't give anyone a key to my house. My home was my sanctuary, I rarely invited anyone over. I preferred going out in public, or at the other person's spot, instead of my own. Darius, didn't even have a key. I planned on giving him one, after we got married. Taking a deep breathe, I put the gun in my bag using my thumb and index finger. Whoever it was, was in for a surprise.

As I climbed my building staircase, the knot in my stomach grew wider and wider. Suddenly, I realized my stressful day was only going to get worse. When I reached my front door, I saw a black bag on the floor with a note attached to front. It read:

Dear Fatty,

I'm sorry about the other day. You know you're my everything. My future wife, and mother of my children. I shouldn't have spoken to you the way I did. I'm sorry. Look inside the bag, I bought you something special, to let you know just how much I love and miss you. There's more waiting for you, on the other side of the door.

Love Darius.

The note was sweet and everything, but how did

he get inside my house? I'm sure, I didn't give him a key. After the argument we had the other day, he didn't call, which really surprised me. Even though, I wasn't sure where we stood, I thought about calling him, practically every second of the day. But decided against it, because I wasn't about to teach him, his behavior was okay. His silence made me feel relieved, I didn't give him full access to my place. The other day had me second guessing our relationship, because I couldn't, and didn't fight.

Reading the note again, I dropped my shoulders, rolled my neck slowly, and realized none of that mattered now, because apparently, swatting my hands, and biting my tongue worked. Since he felt bad enough to arrange such a sweet apology.

I peered down at the bag, sitting in front of my feet. I couldn't help wondering if it was finally the ring, I'd been waiting for? I held my breath, and my pulse quickened, as I eagerly searched inside.

"Lingerie?" I said, letting out a sigh.

I guess, money wasn't what it used to be. I picked up the bag, and walked inside.

"Oh my god, baby." I squealed, holding my chest.

Darius had completely out done himself. There was an assortment of white candles arranged throughout my living room. Joe's I Wanna Know was playing in the background, and petals were scattered on the floor, but he was no where to be found. I dropped the bag and searched for him in my future baby's bedroom, and my own, but didn't find him. I could see the master bathroom door was open, from my bedroom doorway. I walked inside, and found him standing in nothing but a white towel with a glass of champagne in his hand. Slung over his arm was a towel and luffa. The bath water was drawn, and I could see he had my favorite body wash and lotion sitting on the ledge of the tub. I couldn't help noticing how delicious he looked.

"Welcome home." he said, flashing those dimples I love while surveying my body.

"Hi baby. You did all this for me?"

"Of course, I did. You deserve it." He said, but he seemed distracted.

"Babe. Did someone steal your shit. I left a bag and note in front of the door?" He asked, cracking his knuckles. He was gearing up to fight.

"No, honey. I got it. Thank you." I said readily, not wanting him to blow up again.

Maybe he was irritated, but not upset. Either way, I wanted to keep him calm, whenever I could. The fight changed something inside me. It was like I was waiting for the monster to show up again. I wanted to ask, how he got inside my apartment, but it didn't seem like the right time. So, I decided to ask later.

"Let me take care of you." He said, proceeding to undress me from head to toe.

Exhausted, I let him. Our problems could wait, for now. I stepped into the bathtub, and relaxed for the first time all day. I was nice absorbing the moment. At first, we sat quietly, as he worked out all the kinks in my neck and shoulders. Then, I asked the huge question looming in the room.

"Did you fix your business problem, baby?" He must have, why else would he be in such a good mood?

"I thought you'd never ask."

"Daddy's got everything figured out." He said, kissing the back of my neck.

"Hmm, that feels good. Tell me everything."

"Are you sure you want to know?" He said, stalling with a smile in his voice.

"Boy don't play. Tell me, what's up."

"Well, my dad passed away, last week."

Shocked. I spun around in the tub, splashing him in the face.

"Damn. Babe. Watch out." He said, falling back laughing.

"Excuse me?"

"Did I hear you correctly. Your dad dying is good news?" I knew my face looked crazy. But I couldn't help it. I was genuinely shocked. I couldn't believe what he was saying. Was he really happy his dad was dead? I knew Darius put on a strong face, but I would've at least expected him to be a little sad.

"Look. I'm not happy the man is dead. I'm happy, I found a solution to our problems. So chill."

"How's that?" I asked, with raised eyebrows.

"My dad didn't flash his money, but I know he wasn't broke. He was all about his paper. There's no way he didn't have a fat life insurance policy somewhere. He was always teaching me and Marcus to save half of what we earned, and shit like that. Plus, I got a phone call today, telling me to meet with his lawyer tomorrow about his will. His death was a blessing in disguise. I needed 250 grand, right around the time he crocks. So, from where I'm standing, it looks like he was watching over me, without even knowing it? Damn, babe. I thought you'd be happy." He said, throwing his hands up.

Honestly, happy was the last emotion I'd use to describe how I felt, at the moment. I understood, Darius needed the money to stay out of jail.

24

Obviously, I didn't want him getting arrested. But, it would be wrong for me to jump up and down, over a man's death. I've never met his dad, or anyone else in his family, now that I think about it. So hearing about his death, before hearing stories about Christmas or birthdays, seemed off.

"Honey. Of course, I'm happy." I lied. I knew better than to stifle his happiness. Besides, I didn't want to mess up the good vibe we had going.

"Fatty, you're a horrible liar. What's the problem?" He said, sitting on the side of the tub with his arms crossed.

"I don't know. I don't want to be happy about someone dying. It's not right. It almost feels evil."

"Evil? You think, I'm a bad guy?" He asked, looking hurt.

"Of course not. Don't be silly. I know you're a good man. I wouldn't be with you, if I thought you weren't. I just don't know what to think about the whole situation."

Dropping his towel, he joined me in the tub. I turned around, and placed my head on the front of his shoulder.

"I'll tell you what to think." He said, rubbing the center of my sweet spot.

"Think about what kind of dress you'll be wearing, when we walk down the isle, because I'm not going anywhere."

I enveloped the warm sensation taking over my body, because I wanted to believe every word, dripping from his lips. I placed my negative thoughts in box, deep inside the depths of my mind.

"Go on." I said, lost in the dream.

Rubbing my belly, he went on. "You should also rethink your digs. Since, you'll be too big to wear those skinny jeans, and cute clothes you like. I'm going to have you woddeling around this joint soon."

"Oh. Is that right?" I said, turning around, looking deeply into his eyes.

"Darius. Don't lie to me, if you don't mean it. I want to know the truth."

"I'm serious as a heart attack." He said, pulling me onto his manhood.

I wasn't getting any sleep tonight. That was for damn sure. He had me so open, I forgot to ask about his accomplice threatening to squeal.

Chapter Four

I threw my napkin on the bistro table. I was pissed. I stopped myself from cussing out the waitress. Even though, she technically didn't do anything wrong. Besides annoy the hell out of me. Since, she came to my table at least four times within the last twenty minutes, asking if I was ready to order. I told her non-listening behind, I would call her when I was ready. But apparently, she didn't understand English very well. Even though, she looked like a so called all American girl, whatever the hell that means?

"Ma'am, we really need this table, if you're not going to order something soon." She returned.

Grabbing the sides of the table, I took a deep breathe, and exhaled. I needed to calm down, because I really wanted to scream. Truth be told, she had every right to keep coming back. The place was jam packed. People were rushing to grab a bite to eat, before heading back to work. I understood, everyone needed to get paid, especially minimum waged workers. Unfortunately, the state didn't pay me much better than them. So, I couldn't afford to order expensive lunches to eat alone. My real problem was dumb ass, Darius. Not her. He was supposed to be here over an hour ago. At first, I waited outside, hoping his car would pull into the parking lot soon, but then it started to rain. So I decided to take a seat.

"Ma'am." she said, disturbing my thoughts.

"We need this table."

"Fine." I said, gathering my things to leave.

Darius definitely had some explaining to do. If he wasn't dead, incarcerated, or in the hospital. I truly felt sorry for his ass, because I'm ready to set it off. I understood, he had a lot on his mind, but that was no excuse to treat me bad. I planned on giving him more than a piece of my mind. Because, this madness had to stop. I didn't know who he thought he was, standing me up. Sitting in the middle of the restaurant alone wasn't only annoying, it was embarrassing.

"What the hell is the problem now?" I said, aloud.

As I pulled into my complex, I could see his car in my reserved parking space, I paid extra for every month. Begrudgingly, I found an inconvenient place to park far away from my front door. I expected a damn good excuse, because I was more than tired of his bullshit. How could we start a family, if I couldn't even count on him showing up for lunch? Why couldn't he be the responsible business man, I met two years ago? If I was honest with myself, I could admit secretly I hoped the candles, music, and lingerie was a sign the old Darius was back. But obviously, his butt wasn't ready to return. Since the dumb shit kept on rolling.

At the top of the staircase, there was no Darius. This fool had to be sitting in my apartment. I knew I should have asked how he got into my place, the last time he was over. Now I had to deal with these surprise pop ups. Plus, he had the audacity to kick me out of his spot. Meanwhile he had full access to mine. Uh uh, things had to change. I told him, as soon as we met, I didn't want to move in together without being married. He was mad at first, but I thought he understood, and got over it. Of course, he called me crazy, since we had sex, and were always together. I didn't want him having a key to my place, until I had a commitment. Somehow the terms of our relationship changed, without me knowing. I had to reset everything, before shit got too far out of hand.

With my attitude fully intact, I threw open the front door, ready to duke it out. Immediately, I realized I had a much bigger problem than I expected. Darius was slumped in front of my suede couch with a bottle of Jack tightly gripped in his hand. Instantly, my eyes popped open, I dropped everything, and cupped my mouth in shock. He looked a hot mess. The rims of his eyes were red, and the lids were swollen, it appeared he'd been crying.

"Baby. What's the matter?" I said, rushing over to see what was wrong.

"Fuck that nigga. Fuck em. I hope his ass is frying, where ever he is." He said, slurring his words, while trying to stand up.

"Sit down baby. Relax. Tell me what's wrong." I said, pushing his shoulders down.

"The fuck you think? That nigga don't love me. He never did. Nobody gives a fuck about Darius. It's Marcus they love." He said, punching himself in the face.

"Stop it. What the hell are you doing?"I screamed. I'd never seen him like this before. He looked so broken, and confused. What the hell was he drinking? Lighter fluid. I couldn't believe my eyes. He never acted this way. Darius was always strong and well put together. I didn't know the person, in front of me, or where they came from.

"What do you care? You don't care about me. You just want a baby. You don't love me." He said, beginning to cry. He words trailed off, but I got the gist. My baby had finally cracked under the pressure. I held him tightly against my breast, as he cried it out. I didn't know what else to do. But I knew one thing, I wasn't going to abandon him, during his time of need. I knew exactly what it felt like to be alone in this world, full of opportunists and vultures ready to feast on you in a vulnerable moment. I was determined to be the woman he needed me to be no matter what. We were going to make it through whatever was causing him to crack up like this. He was more than my man, he was the only family I had besides, Tasha. Eventually, his tears stopped falling, and it felt safe to break the silence.

"Did Eddie take the deal? Is that why you're upset, baby?" I asked, gently.

"No. Not yet. But he will."

"Don't say that. We don't know that yet."

"You're so fucking stupid. Wake up. I can't come up with the money. It's over. I'm going to jail." He snapped.

"We don't know that. Stop speaking against yourself. Let's stay positive. What did his lawyer say?" I said, choosing to ignore the daggers he threw at me. It must be the sauce talking, not him.

"He said, my dad doesn't give a fuck about me. He didn't leave me shit. Is that what you want to hear?" He said, staggering onto his feet. He tilted his head back, and took another swig. I wanted to stop him, but my intuition told me not to. One wrong move, and he'd be swing on me, instead of himself.

"My dad, didn't leave me shit. But, he left $500,000 to my brother. He could have split it

31

down the middle. Half is exactly what I needed. But no. You know what the muthafucker left me? A bible. A motherfucking bible." He said, laughing so hard it brought him to tears.

"Can you believe that shit? I'm his oldest son. I'm his goddamn junior. Not Marcus. I'm his fucking son too. What about me?" He roared, as if I was his dad, instead of his girl. Stumbling back, he fell onto his left leg and took another drink.

"Marcus doesn't even need the shit. He's a fucking doctor."

Quietly, I watched on the couch as he spiraled into a dark place, I didn't want to visit. I had no idea where the night was headed. I'd learned more about him, his father, and his brother, than I ever knew before. Every time, I tried to ask him about his family in the past, he would change the subject. I figured, it was too painful to talk about like parts of my childhood. I totally understood wanting to move up and foreword.

Punching, nothing but air, he started screaming, "I'm sorry. I didn't meant it." over and over again.

"Baby, what did you do? Why are you sorry." Was all I could get out from across the room. I stayed planted on the couch as tears of sadness and frustration streamed from my eyes. I wanted to hold him, and tell him everything was going to be okay, but I was too afraid. I didn't know what he would do next. He fell onto his knees, and cried in the middle of my living room floor. I could tell he was exhausted. Slowly, I slid onto the floor in front of the couch. I wanted him to know he wasn't alone.

"Tell me what happened baby. I want to help you feel better. Let it out."

"I killed him."

I sucked in a deep breathe, and held it. I didn't want to show him, how much what he said, shocked and frightened me. I knew Darius committed white collar crimes. But murder. It took me over a year to accept he stole financial information from dead people and the elderly. But murder, I didn't think I could swallow. I wasn't prepared to hear the words coming out of his mouth. His eyes were surveying my reaction, they felt like beams burning into my skin. Gradually, I let my chest fall. Hoping my surprise didn't register on my face. I didn't say anything. I just waited for him to continue, as he set cradling his head in his hands.

"I was just a little kid. I don't know how it happened." He paused, and looked at me like he was deciding whether to continue. The truth was, he had no choice, because the words had already been spoken. He'd have to tell me now or later, because, never was no longer an option.

"We were supposed to stay inside, but I didn't listen. I snuck out anyway, without my parent's permission."

"Fuck. Why didn't I listen." He continued with hot streams running down his face.

"Even then, he was the better son. All my parents talked about was Marcus is so smart, Marcus is going to follow in Big D's footsteps, Why can't Darius be more like Marcus? The shit never stopped. No matter what I did. I could never be better than him. So, I stopped trying. If they didn't want to see the good in me, I'd show them how bad I could be."

In that moment, I realized I didn't want him to continue. There was no doubt in my mind Darius was the man for me. But our relationship wasn't the same after his explosion the other day. I still loved him, but my view of him was different. He no longer was my pillar of strength. Seeing him out of control and fragile, woke me up to reality. I built him up in my mind. His ability to survive in difficult situations hooked me to him. I unfairly made him out to be a super hero, because I needed one at the time. Now, he needed me. I wasn't sure if I could be there for him in the same way, because his problems were so huge, and larger than life, but I was going to try. I continued to listen to his confession, and prayed I could handle whatever he was going to say next.

"Eric loved me. He loved everyone, but

especially me. He looked at me like I was super human. Everywhere I went, he wanted to go. He was my sidekick, until that night. Everyone wanted to go to the fair, including me, but my parents said no. Instead of listening, I woke up, grabbed my bag, full of soda and snacks I prepared earlier, and headed out. Unfortunately, Eric woke up before I could get out the window. He wanted to come along. I was just a kid, too. I was thirteen years old. I just wanted to have fun with everyone else. I didn't want anyone to get hurt. I tried to tell him he was too little and needed to stay. But he was persistent like most 7 years old. He wouldn't take no for an answer. He put on his shoes, because he wanted to go too. He was so excited to go with his big brother. If he only he knew, what I had planned for him. I told him to be quiet, so we didn't wake up the rest of the house. Marcus was asleep in the room too. I didn't want Jesus himself to wake up. Unfortunately, the piece of shit stayed asleep. God, why didn't he wake up? If anyone shouldn't be here, it was him, not Eric. He could have stopped me. God, why didn't he stop me."

I held myself so tightly, my fingers began to tingle. I couldn't process what he was saying. Eric? Who the hell was Eric? And why didn't he tell me about him sooner? Darius never told me he had another brother until tonight? He told me about Marcus, his mom, and his dad. I could tell the conversation was headed in a dark direction. I

35

wanted him to stop. It seemed like talking about it helped him control his emotions. So, there was no way, I was going to interrupt.

"We had a blast at the fair. We ate Now or Laters, Cry Babies, Kit Kats, and drank grape soda all night. Eric said, he never had so much fun. It was really a night to remember." He eyes teared up and he took a breathe. It was obviously hard for him to continue.

"We walked home. It must have been at least 11 o'clock. Eric kept lagging behind. I was tired, I kept telling him to catch up. I'd stop for a few seconds, but didn't carry him. Instead, I let him fall behind. Eventually, we reached the train tracks. It was only two blocks from our house. He was so far behind, I could barely see him. By the time, I heard the sound of the train. I realized I couldn't see him anymore. I tried to reach him. I turned back around." Streams started running down the length of his face. I tried to put my arms around him, but he pulled back.

"Damn it. Fatty. I need to say this. I turned back around. I ran as fast as I could. But he was gone. The train drug him for miles. When I got back, he was nothing but broken bones, cartilage, and mangled flesh. It was my fault. They were right. I'm a piss of shit." Darius started hitting the sides of his face. He completely lost. I ran to him, forcing my arms around him. If he was going to hurt himself,

he could hit me too. I wasn't about watch him self
destruct anymore. Luckily, as soon as I did, he
stopped. I held him for the rest of the night, until he
fell asleep.

Chapter Five

I hardly got any sleep. Seeing Darius fall to pieces in front of my eyes, really woke me up to some hardcore truths. All this time, he'd been focused on me, without taking care of himself. He bought my car, paid my rent, and took me shopping amongst other things while carrying such a heavy burden alone. Meanwhile, he was living in his own personal hell, and I wasn't even aware. What type of partner was I, if I didn't even know he was suffering? I was disgusted with myself. I should have known he needed me. I couldn't help feeling selfish, which was why I was going to doing everything in my power to make it up to him.

As soon as the sun peeked over the clouds, I was zipping around the house. All morning, I'd been cleaning and rearranging furniture to clear my mind. I was determined to find a solution to his problems before he woke up. He'd been a pillar of strength for me in the past. Now it was my turn to do the same for him. If outside influences were going to try to bring my baby down, I'd have to dilute their effects by being twice as positive, and encouraging. He obviously needed my help keeping his head above water. So, that was exactly what I was going to do. After spending a few hours thinking about everything that's transpired over the last few weeks, I found a good solution to our problems. I just hoped he would go along with my plan.

I placed a fresh pair of folded black lounge pants and a crisp white tee shirt on the foot of the bed, before heading back to the kitchen. He was still nestled in dream world, unaware of what I had planned for him once he woke up. The smoked ham I was sizzling in a cast iron skillet, while I scrambled four eggs in the pan next door. I had a bowl of pancake batter resting on the counter top, too. It would be ready to throw on the hot griddle as soon as he walked into the kitchen. Today was going to be a good day for him no matter what. Nothing was going to ruin it, if I had anything to say about it.

"Hmm, what's that smell?" He asked, walking into the room while rubbing his belly.

"Breakfast for a king of course. I've got smoked ham, scrambled eggs, and buttermilk pancakes on the way." I said, pouring the pancake batter onto the hot griddle. I jogged over, and placed a soft kiss on his lips. Then asked, "How'd you sleep?"

"Damn, baby. I knew, I had good taste." He said, showing off his deep dimples. He wrapped his arm around my waist, and pulled me into a deep kiss. I knew my baby was grateful without him saying a word. His sweet kiss was all the thanks I needed. I quickly ran around the breakfast bar to flip the pancakes before they burned.

"Babe, about last night."

"Uh uh, today is a new day. Do you really want to talk about last night?" I said, placing his food and a glass of orange juice in front of him, with a skeptical look on my face.

He smiled at me from the bar and said, "You're amazing, girl. I don't know how I got so lucky."

"We're meant to be together. Luck has nothing to do with it."

Looking at him I could see, he was in a much better mood. I didn't want to drag down the day by focusing on last night. As far as, I was concerned yesterday was dead, gone, and irrelevant. There was no point in talking about it now. We just needed to move on, and forward.

"I don't want to talk about the past, but I do want to discuss our future. You up for it?" I asked, not wanting to push to soon.

"Shoot."

"Well, I've been thinking about our predicament. I know you have a potentially pending case we can stop by paying Eddie. But that doesn't look possible at the moment. So, I've been thinking of alternative plans. I think I have a good one, that can keep us together and you out of jail."

"Did I wake up in heaven? Because you're answering all my prayers without me even asking. He said, laughing.

"Shush. I'm serious." I said, placing my finger over his lips.

"We may not have money at the moment, but he have time, and a heads up. So, lets make the best of it. We could sell everything. Your house, my car, our clothes, everything but a few necessity items. Then, we can clear out our accounts. Before heading out of town. I know I've been waiting to have a little Darius for the longest, but not if that means I have to lose you. Having you home with me is more important than anything else. We will need to get married though. So if worse case scenario happens, we wouldn't have to testify against each other.

Darius sat back, and contemplated what I said. I couldn't tell from his expression what he was thinking. I just crossed my fingers and hoped he would think it was a good plan. He got up from the bar stool, and grabbed both of my hands.

"Fatima, I appreciate you trying to help fix the situation. I really do. I couldn't ask for more. But my problems arc little more complicated than that. I can't just get up and leave. The type of business I do, isn't hard to track, when somebody has the inside scoop. Plus, there are cameras on practically every street corner these days. Where could we go without anyone seeing us get there. The camera nowadays are so good they can count the money in your hands from across the room."

Dropping my shoulders, I began to shed a few tears. I knew my idea was a stretch, but I couldn't think of anything else to do. Darius swept away the tears on my cheek and held me close. For the first time in awhile, I allowed myself to relax in his embrace.

"I don't want you worry about us, and definitely not me. I'm may have been down for a minute, but I'm still the man. I can take care of us. You don't have to worry. I've found a solution to our problem, but you'll have to keep an opened mind." I raised my forehead off his shoulders, eager to hear his plan.

"Tell me. We have to do something. We can't just sit on our hands, because I don't know what I'd do, if you weren't home with me." Darius pecked my lips and led me to the living room couch. We both set down while he held my hands.

"I'll need your support to make this plan work. But, I'm just not sure you'll agree to help me." He said, rubbing his forehead with one hand.

"Are you crazy. Have I not proven, I'm here for you enough? Of course, I'll help. I'll do anything to keep you safe, and at home. Now tell me."

"I'm not sure you can, because you're not about this life. You didn't even want to be with me when I told you about my business. It almost tore us apart. I don't know if you can handle doing what it takes to get me out of this situation.

"Darius, I don't know what to tell you. I've accepted your business and way of life, which is why I'm still sitting here. I'm older and wiser now. I understand life isn't fairy dust and unicorns. Sometimes you have to step outside the lines to get what you need. I get that now. You're my family. If I have to make sacrifices in the short term to have you in the long term, so be it. I'll do whatever it takes to keep you home. So we can have the family we've always wanted.

"Good. Because I have a fail proof plan, but you're gonna have to be smart enough to think outside the box. You can't be like most women who operate off of emotion. You'll have to do what it takes to get us out of this situation. I know you have a good head on your shoulders. I'm just not sure, if you trust me.

"Stop slow playing Darius. Of course, I trust you. Just tell me what I can do to help."

"We can't get 250 G's in two months, because I'm too hot right now. I can't risk getting caught. And nobody wants to do business with me for obvious reason. Which is why, my dad's life insurance policy was my last shot."

"Right."

"Well, I've got a back a plan."

"Go on."

"Marcus has 500 G's coming in about the same time. He doesn't know anything about me, but I know plenty about him. I've done a thorough background check on him. And my brother isn't hurting for money."

"So, you"re going to ask him for your half?"

"No. You are."

"I am? He doesn't even know me."

"That's why it's perfect. Here me out."

"Marcus is a chump. He doesn't know shit about shit. The only thing he's ever known is how to read a book. The kid has no street smarts or common sense. I think his ass is autistic, or something. Point is. We can easily con him out of his money."

"How can we con him? I don't know anything about conning somebody. Plus, I don't feel comfortable doing that."

"So, you won't do anything for us to be together."

"Darius. That's not what I said."

"Then what are you saying?" Darius was

starring me down. He was disappointed in my response. I just didn't know what to say, because I wasn't expecting him to bring up his brother. I wasn't lying when I said, I'd do anything for us to be together. I just didn't see how us both committing crimes, would stop him from getting arrested.

"I can't commit crimes. I'm a school teacher. That would ruin my career, if I got caught. Plus I don't see how me becoming a criminal, keeps you out of jail.

"Fatty, you're my girl. I would never ask you to do anything that could get you arrested." Relived, I let out a heavy sigh.

"I don't know how to say this. So, I'm just going to come out with it. I need you to hustle my brother."

"Hustle him? Hustle him. You mean, you want me to have sex with your brother?

"I mean, I want you to get what we need, however you can. If that means sex okay, but of course, any other way would be better."

I just sat there with my mouth open. I didn't have any words to express how I felt. I just sat there and stared at him.

"Look. I know it's a lot to take in. I wouldn't ask, if there was any other way. Believe me. I don't want my girl to be with anyone else, but this is the only way for us to have what we want. After you get the money, I'll be free. We can get married, and have the baby you've always wanted. Just think about it. I know, you'll make the right decision.

"I'm going to wash up. You can join me if you want." Darius stood up and walked towards the bathroom. Stunned. I sat on the couch, alone, trying to figure out how my life became such a mess. Never in a million years did I think Darius would ask me to sleep with another man, let alone his own brother.

Chapter Six

Driving to Tasha's house seemed like a trip around the world, since it felt like the earth stopped spinning, and the sun didn't come out, after what Darius asked me to do. Apart of me, felt like he was being the logical go getter, I fell in love with several years ago. It sounds crazy on the surface, but what he said did make a lot of sense. There was no way to keep him with me, if we couldn't come up the 250 grand. Hell, I wouldn't take the wrap for free if I was Eddie, either. Besides, his brother got more than his share of their father's life insurance policy. The fact his dad chose to punish him, even in death, for a mistake he made as a child was disgusting in my opinion. He should have split everything down the middle, instead of leaving Marcus everything. Plus, the bible was an unnecessary fuck you to boot. I could only assume, Darius thought we'd live happily ever after, if I went along with his plan. But of course, that was wishful thinking because life never goes according to plan.

I hated to admit it, but I understood where he was coming from. Darius was just being his typical analytical self. I used to love the fact he was unemotional and direct, when making important decisions. Everything usually turned out good, because of his unique perspective on things. I actually thought, his unemotional view of the world was more balanced than my sometimes fanciful way of thinking. But now, it was coming back to bite me on the ass. I didn't know what to do. A large part of me couldn't believe he loved me, if he'd let me sleep with another man, regardless of the situation. Because we could always start where we left off, if he did get arrested. Had I known, he was going to ask me to do something so crazy, I wouldn't have went on about being willing to do anything to keep him out of jail. Now, I felt obligated to follow through.

I sat inside my car in front of Tasha's apartment and spaced out for a bit. My mind was overdue for a break. The kids were running and playing outside, like they were having the time of their life. Octavia was chasing DeMarcus and Nikki with a water hose, while I let my thoughts roam to a better place. I smiled enviously, as I watched them play freely. If only I could leave my problems behind, and join them. I could see Tasha sitting on the porch beating a pack of cigarettes against her palm. It didn't look like she was in a good mood from were I was sitting, which was strange because she usually was.

"Your highness, are you going to join me on the porch." She asked, dramatically taking a bow.

"I was just admiring the kids. I'm right behind you." I said, grabbing my purse and water bottle.

We settled into our sits on her front porch. Tasha popped a fresh Newport 100 in her mouth, as we watched them play. It was a typical gorgeous June summer day. Neighbors were out playing bones, drinking beer, bumping music, and hanging out. Witnessing the carefree spirit around me only made me feel worse. I couldn't help wondering how the hell things got so bad?

"What's the matter? Darius didn't buy you another car?" Tasha laughed, sarcastically.

I hated when Tasha acted like my life was a bed of roses. Yes, I didn't have three children that I raised alone, but that was intentional, not accidental. I could have easily been her, if I focused on getting ahead, instead of getting my education. Single mother's like her drove me crazy with their tiny violins and sob stories. True. Tasha had been through some things, but I had too. She should be trying to figure out how to get a job. Instead of what my man was or wasn't doing for me. It really shouldn't have been any of her concern.

"Girl, how you been? You know I'm just a little tipsy. I don't mean no harm."

I cut my eyes at her, cleared my throat and said, "Things have been a little rough lately. I was hoping to get some advice from my sister. But, if you're too lit to talk. Let me know, I have no problem moving around."

"Go ahead girl, I'm sorry. It ain't nothing but the devil in this cup, causing me to act like that. I got it together now." She said, straightening her shirt, and sitting up right.

"Darius has been going through somethings. I failed to mention he was being blackmailed, the last time I saw you. That's why he lost it the other day. One of his partners, got arrested recently, and he is threatening to tell his business, if he doesn't come up with some serious cash."

Tasha grabbed her stomach and fell over laughing. She wiped away tears with the back of her hand, she was cracking up so much. Catching her breath she said, "Child, everybody knows Darius's ain't nobody's boss, or business man. You're the only fool dense enough to believe anything said to you. The whole city knows he is a hustler in a suit and tie, your dumb ass is the only one out of the loop. I swear, you're as late as a ho on Sunday morning. I been knowing the business. I'm just glad your ass, finally decided to tell me the truth."

I watched, as someone I consider my sister, made light of my situation. I thought about my limited resources, and my eyes began to sting. Tasha and Darius were my support system, but neither were being very good to me at the moment. I came over expecting her to offer me some sound advice and direction. If I knew she was going to be so ruthless and cold, I would have saved my gas and stayed home. Losing my man, dream, and way of life was bad enough, without having her laugh about it. So I gathered my things to leave. I wasn't about to let her make my already difficult situation worse.

"Fatima … Fatima? Where are you going girl? You can't take a joke? She said, tugging on my wrist.

"I don't have time for games, today. If you're not going to be my sister by helping me, I'm gonna leave. I don't have time for your mess."

Tasha cleared her throat, and patted the chair next to her. "Fatima, your right. I shouldn't be making fun of you. I won't drink anything until we figure this situation out." I looked at her sideways, but sat down.

To my surprise, Tasha leaned towards me, and took another sip of her drink. Why she thought I cared, I don't know, but she was definitely doing it to get under my skin, which is why I didn't give her a reaction. I just looked at her like the fool, she was acting like. There was no way, I was wasting my precious energy, on a stupid argument. Especially, since I didn't even know what she was upset about.

"You know what your problem is?" She said, with a grin on her face.

"You're desperate. You're simply too damn desperate. You're always looking for someone to love and comfort you. But, you never think about anybody else. I'm tired of being your free sounding board. You need to start paying me to listen to your dumb ass problems.

At this point, I didn't understand why we're friends, if she felt this way. Yeah, she'd been drinking, but she meant what she was saying. The relief she held in her eyes, told me she had been wanting to tell me off, for awhile. So I wasn't going to stop her. I wanted to know what my so called friend really thought about me.

"And another thing. Darius doesn't give a damn about you, or anybody else. You're just too dumb to see you're dancing with the devil. His ass is crazy, and always has been. Why can't you get that through your thick head. You're like an expensive accessory to him." She said laughing.

"You're just another thing he uses to make other guys around him jealous and envious of his position. How else could he keep up with his large and in charge persona, without any real qualifications or pedigree. He'd just be another nigga with a dream. And stop, talking about this picket fence bullshit too. If he wanted to give you a child, you'd have one by now.

Infuriated, I slapped the solo cup out of her

hand. I wasn't about to let her talk about me, and my baby like she lost her damn mind. I didn't have any idea how to fight. But I was going to beat her ass. I stepped into her personal space. And she bucked back. So we were literally tit-tee to tit-tee.

"Oh. So you think you can whop me Saint Mary?" She laughed, standing inches from my face.

"You can get mad all you want. But believe me. I know what I'm talking about. Actually, now that I think about it. You're not dumb. His ass just has you dick-matized. He still don't love you, though. A nigga will stick his dick in just about anything. So, don't get your hopes up. He's just taking advantage, because you're a pretty simpleton, that is easy to keep in line."

SCREECH!

The sound of screeching tires and clashing metal, disturbed us. We both spun around, and ran into the front yard. A blue sedan crashed into a parked car up the street. I quickly did a head count. After remembering kids were playing in the yard while we were busy arguing like idiots. Immediately, I noticed DeMarcus was missing.

"DeMarcus, DeMarcus!" I screamed, frantically. Tasha did too.

Gripping my hair, I turned in every direction, but didn't see him. Nikki and Octavia pointed up the street, saying the car got him. Tasha and I, both ran up the street, and found him laying limp on the ground. She fell to her knees, and cried rocking her baby back and forth. My adrenaline was pumping so fast. I didn't cry or ask what happened. Instead, I took off towards the house. I threw Octavia and Nikki in the front passenger seat, and drove back to scene of the accident. I could hear sirens approaching, but I didn't care about them or the people huddled around us. I told Tasha to get in the back with DeMarcus, and she did, without hesitation.

Just like that, everything changed. I didn't even know why Tasha was so mad at me, or why I sat there listening to her insult me, and everyone I love. But none of that mattered now. The only thing I cared about was taking care of an innocent little boy, who was injured, in my back seat. I had to do everything I could to make sure he was okay. I called the hospital on my way over, as I rushed to the emergency room. Silently I prayed for hundredth time today, that everything would turn out alright.

Chapter Seven

As soon as I pulled into the emergency room driveway, they grabbed DeMarcus, and put him on a gurney that seemed to envelop his tiny body. Two medical transporters rushed him behind the emergency room double doors, and instructed us to wait in the lobby. Tasha filled out the necessary paperwork at the front desk, while I watched Nikki and Octavia. Surprisingly, there wasn't a lot of people waiting along side us. The girls played with toys and books laid out for kids in the middle of the room. They both asked about their little brother, but were oblivious to the severity of the situation. I tried to watch the television hanging in the corner of the room, but the day's events kept preventing me from processing what was on the screen.

I couldn't stop thinking about DeMarcus, and how he wouldn't be in this situation, if I had left Tasha's house when I wanted to the first time. Now that I think about it, Tasha wouldn't be a complete mess right now, and we probably wouldn't have fought, if I had just stayed home.

She finished up at the front desk, then sat down several sits away from me. I wanted to be there for her, because she hadn't stopped crying since they took him back. Our argument shouldn't have been relevant now, but apparently it still was, because neither of us said a word to each other after they whisked him away. I didn't initiate a conversation, because I had no desire to over step my bounds. I figured she purposely created a large space between us because she didn't want to be bothered with me. Still, I wasn't going home until, I knew DeMarcus was okay. Whether she liked it or not. So I bit my nails, and waited nervously for the hospital attendee to invite us back. She was definitely wrong for what she said to me earlier, but I wasn't going to make a big deal out of the situation. Since I couldn't imagine being in her position. If my child got hurt on my watch, I wouldn't be able to forgive myself.

"Tasha Stewart." A burly woman said, entering the waiting room.

Tasha wiped away her tears, and took the girls hands. I was only a step behind them.

"What are you doing?" She said, glaring over her shoulder at me.

"What am I doing? She couldn't be serious. I want to support you, and make sure my nephew is okay."

Tasha let go of the girl's hands, and spun around on her heels. "After all I said today. You still don't get it. Everything isn't about you. Fatima. Nothing happened to you. My son is the one that is hurt. You don't belong here. His not your child, nephew, or anything else. I don't want your help. Just leave.

Your Ms. Do Right attitude is annoying as hell, and not needed."

I looked to my left and right in disbelief. She couldn't be talking to me. When the hell, did I become her enemy. I had no interest in being the center of attention. I dedicated several of my days off to taking care of her kids, especially DeMarcus. Every part of me wanted to act a fool. But how could I? Technically I wasn't family. I loved Tasha and her kids. For years I considered them my family. I bought them things, babysat whenever she needed, and drove her around whenever her car broke down. But apparently, I was just some idiot she was taking advantage of and using.

"Excuse me ma'am. Can I speak with you for a moment?" The attendee asked, interrupting her speech. She pulled her aside to talk. I couldn't make out what she was saying, because she held a clip board in front of her mouth, and spoke softly. However, I could get the gist of the conversation, by piecing together Tasha's responses. Apparently, DeMarcus needed a blood transfusion. From what I could gather. Apparently, Tasha and the girls weren't a match. It sounded like the attendee was suggesting, I stay and get tested. I volunteered myself, just in case my hunch was correct.

"I'll give you whatever you need, if it will help DeMarcus."

"Bitch are you dumb. Get the hell out of here. I got this. Just leave." Tasha grabbed the girls, and pushed passed the attendee.

Defeated, I drug myself to my car in the emergency room parking lot. I was dumbfounded by how she was treating me. My mind was such a convoluted mess, I just stared blankly as people went in and out of the sliding glass doors. I thought about calling Darius, but I didn't want to hear about him and his endless list of problems. So I decided against it. He had been blowing up my phone the entire time, I was at Tasha's. But I kept sending him to voice mail. The last thing I wanted to think about was getting myself into another complicated situation. When I was already in the middle of an argument.

"What the hell is going on?" I said aloud, perplexed.

Quietly, I stepped out of my driver's side door, and slowly closed it behind me. Then, I bent down, and made my way around the car. It had been several hours since we arrived. There were only a few cars in the parking lot, and most were occupied by hospital staff. The parking lot was dimly lit. I squinted, and attempted to look around the line of bushes standing next to my car, but couldn't see very well. I needed to move in closer. I camouflaged myself as best I could, and moved through the lot like a highly skilled ninja. If my eyes weren't playing tricks on me, there was a Darius look-a-like entering the hospital. When I watched him jog through the emergency room entrance, negative thoughts immediately bombarded my mind. But I shook them off. It couldn't have been him. I had to be tripping. What reason would he have to be here?

"What the hell!" I yelled, and shot up from my hidden ninja pose. The bottom of my jeans got soaked by the irrigation system hiding underneath the bushes. Of course it would randomly come on with me standing here. I couldn't help thinking God was being extra funny today. I shook my pants legs, and beat the excess water of my shoes. I needed to get a better look without being seen. I crept to the side of the building, then peered through the slit between the emergency room curtains, just in time to see Tasha running through the back room doors. She really looked awful. Her eyes were swollen and red rimmed. Her usually whipped hair was matted and scattered in the back of her head. Right away I realized, I probably looked no better, after fighting and worrying all day.

Tasha threw her arms around the Darius look-a-like's shoulders, and my breath got caught in my chest. As I watched the two embrace for what felt like forever, beads of sweat began to form around my hairline. I could feel my blood beginning to boil, as I thought about what I could be witnessing.

Could this stranger, holding my so called friend, be my Darius? I tried to push down the emotions rising in my throat, but it felt impossible. Maybe this was the reason, she was being so cruel to me earlier, and didn't want me to stay. After the day I had, I didn't want to rush to conclusions. I needed solid evidence, not a hutch. What could I do to verify it was him? Obviously, I could go in there, but I wasn't about to start up another fight with her. What if I was wrong. Then I'd feel sad, mad, and guilty. I certainly didn't need anymore stress or upset. I got it. I'll search for his car.

My heart quietly begged me to let it go. Darius and Tasha together. It couldn't be possible. I would have known. There was no way, they could have been together without me catching wind of it. Regardless, of my emotional desire to stay in the dark, my mind wouldn't let it go. I was on a mission to catch his ass, if it was him. I was tired of being everybody's fool. As a walked around the lot, I called his phone. It rang a couple of times, then went to voice mail. It's 12 o'clock in the morning. His tail should be home. To my horror, I saw what looked like his 2012 Audi A8. It couldn't be his. I dialed his number again, and slowly stepped towards the side of the black sedan.

"Damn." I wailed to the top of my lungs it was him. I chucked my cell phone through the driver side window, and the alarm began to sound. A tall fat white man yelled in my direction. So, I grabbed my phone and jetted towards my car. How the fuck could he do this to me, after everything I've done for him. How could Tasha, my girl, betray me. I'm such a fool. I hopped in the front seat, revved my engine, and sped out of the parking lot, before the sloppy man could reach me. I was tired of playing the fool. I grabbed my rear view mirror, and saw the pain and misery in my eyes. Silently, I promised myself, never again.

Chapter Eight

I hadn't been home since I found out the news. Instead I paid for a three day room at the The Renaissance. Plus, I turned off my phone. Quit my job. And popped a few pills since finding out my so called life was an incestuous cluster fuck, I created in my naive mind. Darius my fiance, let alone husband? What a fucking joke. To think I actually wanted to have kids with such a piece of shit was both pathetic and disgustingly hilarious. The lies we tell ourselves.

And that bitch, Tasha, was lucky I didn't drag her ass out of the hospital, and into the street. Hurt child or no. She deserved to get her ass beat. As much as I didn't want to admit it. She was right about Darius. She had his crusty ass pegged. If he wanted to marry me, he would have. If he wanted to make me happy. He would have given me the only thing I ever asked for, a child. I took another swig of my drink, and laughed. I had been doing that so much lately, my sides hurt. It was utterly amazing, how bad things had gotten. He actually chose her over me. The bitch had three kids by three different men, and one of them was mine. I never would have thought. Her pussy literally had no bounds.

Yeah. He claimed me in the street. Bought me

things. And on the surface treated me nicely which actually makes it works. Because when I reminisced about the times he said, he wanted to start a family, my fingers start to itch from my bullshit allergy. They itched because every part of me wanted to shot, and stab his ass for every lie he ever told me. To think, he wanted me to help him stay out of jail. The nerve. Meanwhile, he freely Tasha the one thing I wanted the most. There was no way in hell, I was helping his sorry ass. When I thought about bending over backwards to accommodate his needs, and more, I was glad I didn't bring a child into the world. How could I protect a child, if I couldn't even protect myself from these monsters out here today.

I bet his deceitful ass was freaking out, because he couldn't find me. What would he do without his pretty simpleton, as Tasha put it. Now wonder he had no problem asking me to sleep with his brother. He was fucking my soul sister the entire we were together. Why not keep it in the family even more! Them being together explains why she was so happy to hear he flipped out the day Tool called about Eddie threatening to snitch. Her mouth said one thing, but her eyes were jumping with joy when I explained how my nose got busted.

Everything made sense. Tasha knew Darius was a match. Why else would he have been there? They needed his father's blood in order to give him a transfusion, asap. That stupid bitch, knew who his father was all along. Who would concoct a whole story about an imaginary baby daddy who's married with two kids. She was just as sick as his ass.

"Ho? Whatchu doing?" Shana slurred, jarring me out of my thoughts. She stumbled over with Trina and Denise. They all walked across the club to our table. "You came out to party." Shana said, pointing at me. "So come on." She threw her hands up, and started dancing with the others girls.

I didn't want to join. So, I smiled and continued to sip on my drink. I'd been partying with them for the last 24 hours. Every once in awhile we'd chat on Facebook about the wild times we had in college. Shana was the life of the party back in the day. She could get us in the VIP section at any club, and was infamous for streaking down the dorm room halls every time midterms and finals came around. It was like a tradition. Denise on the other hand, was almost the complete opposite. She could be a real drag, but she served a purpose. Some would call her human man repellent. We never had to worry about being swarmed by men. She naturally kept them away. Denise could throw down, and was known for putting bitches to sleep, if things got out of hand. Trina wasn't an old friend. So I couldn't say much about her. All I knew was she gave me Tasha on dubs. As soon as we met, she was telling me about her sex escapades in a climatic fashion, which was enough to turn me off to her. I didn't want another loose trick in my life. One was too many. I hardly said anything to her the entire time we'd been out. I just rolled my eyes, and looked elsewhere, when she started talking.

Out of no where, she yanked me out onto the dance floor. I was too lit to resist. So off I went. She grabbed my waist, and started rubbing her body up against mine. "Get off me." I protested, brushing her off. But she kept popping and dropping various parts of her body. She must have lost her mind. I walked away, but I could fell her on my heels. What the hell did she want?

"Hey, what up." I ignored her, and kept walking. I slid into the booth, and she did too.

"Did I do something wrong?" She asked, wrinkling her forehead.

"I don't know you." I asserted.

"Exactly. Why have you been throwing shade all night, then? You'd think I fucked your man."

"You did." Fell out of my mouth before I could catch the words.

"Is your man Steven?"

"No."

"Q?"

"No."

"Kenny?"

No." I said, throwing my hands up. This girl was already giving me a headache, and this was our first real conversation. At this rate, I better say something, because we'd be here all night, with the amount of men she was naming off.

"How long ago are we talking?"

"You didn't sleep with my man. I don't think you have anyway. You just remind me of someone who did. Recently." I could feel my cheeks heating up on my face. I'm sure she thought I was crazy blaming her for something another female did. If she did think I lost my mind, she didn't show it. But she did start flagging Shana and Denise over. They both staggered over to join us.

"This better be good." Shana said rolling her eyes. She'd been grinding on the same guy all night. It looked like there were heading for the door, as soon as Trina called her over.

"Our friend here has a problem. Trina said, pointing at me.

"Our friend. You'll just met. But what's up." Denise retorted. You could always count on her pointing out the negative, in all situations.

"Yeah. Friend. I said it. Trina raised her brows, waiting for a response, but Denise just sucked her teeth and listened. "She needs our help cashing a whop ass groupon. Her so called girl fucked her man. We should hit her up. Like we used to do tricks back in the day."

All three of them started getting hype. Denise looked especially excited. Any reason to through down was a good reason in her book. I didn't plan on paying Tasha any visits. Doing things like that wasn't part of my style, or personality. But neither was quitting my job, popping pills, clubbing, or half the shit I planned on doing next. Finding out about Darius and Tasha, really fucked me up.

"Who's driving?" Shana said, bouncing her shoulders and throwing her fist.

"I haven't been drinking that much. I'll drive." Trina said, volunteering.

"If we were going anywhere else. I wouldn't have agreed on letting her drive. But oh girl, had a plan to get my self respect back. So how could I deny her. Besides, I had been drinking all night. My car would have been safer in the hands of anyone's, but mine. We were out the club and posted up a few houses down from Tasha house in a hot second. Trina hit the lights, and we quickly began planning.

"I'll throw shit at her car to sound the alarm. Then, one of you grab her ass." Trina suggested.

"That won't work. She doesn't have a car with an alarm. Her old Honda Civic is only for decoration.

It hasn't started up since Jesus was walking." I replied.

"Y'all are over thinking this shit." Shana jumped out the car, and the other two girls followed closely behind her. I crept cautiously behind them, questioning my decision to come out here. It was late, and I really wasn't trying to get arrested. Shana knocked on Tasha's door, then took off towards the side of the house. We all followed her lead. The lights in the living room came on. It was game time. As soon as she opened the door, Denise was on her ass. She had her in a head lock, while Shana and Trina got some licks in. My ass was frozen in place. What the hell did I let myself get into.

"Bitch you better throw a blow." Trina said, egging me on. "This is for you. She didn't fuck my man." Tasha was crying and screaming for them to let her go. I can't lie. I loved seeing her in pain. The bitch deserved it after all she put me through. They stopped hitting her, and she fell to the ground. I got in a few kicks, before spitting on her curled up body. She was in the fetal position. The neighbors lights came on, and we all jetted towards my vehicle laughing. Trina hopped in the front seat. I sat in the passengers side, and the other girls climbed into the back. What the hell was wrong with me? I just jumped someone, I considered family. And it felt so good.

Chapter Nine

Before I could turn the key and press against the door, it flung open. Darius swept me into his large arms and spun me around the living room, as soon as I stepped through the threshold. He was squeezing me so tight it felt like my rib cage was going to burst.

"Oh my god, baby. I've been going out of my mind. Where the fuck have you been? I couldn't eat or sleep. Every time I tried, I pictured you hurt or dead behind some dumpster. I'm so happy you're home." He voice was so high pitched and filled with concern. You would have thought he actually cared about me. Good thing I knew better than to take him at his word. He put me down, swept the curls away from my face, and looked deeply into my eyes. He obviously wanted to know where I'd been. But I wasn't going to give him any respect by answering his questions. He didn't deserve it.

"Well, I'm back. So you don't have anything to worry about." I said, throwing my keys and purse onto the couch. He looked ragged and weighed down with worry. Who would have thought the shoe would be on the other foot so soon. I walked passed him, and into my master bathroom. I desperately needed to wash up after partying nonstop for the last few days. Turning the shower head on, I saw him enter the bathroom by way of my peripheral.

"So you're just going to stroll in here after being gone for the last five days like nothing happened?" He was pissed. I could see a thick vein pulsating on the side of his temple. Oh well. Those are breaks, I thought to myself. I wasn't about to tell him shit. After the lies, he'd been throwing at me during our entire relationship, he didn't deserve an explanation. Especially not from me.

"What do you mean, baby? I just needed a break from all the stress. Everything is better now." I lied, while slipping off the thin sleeves of my dress, and allowing it to fall onto the floor. I had a surprise for him. I knew he would like. I wasn't wearing a bra or panties. He clenched his teeth and balled up his fist just as I expected.

"What the hell has gotten into you? You've been walking around with your pussy blowing in the wind. You want these niggas out here to see your tit-tees and shit too." I had to throw my hair over my head to disguise the smug grin sweeping across my face. It took everything I had, not to bust out laughing, partially because I enjoyed his pain, and partially because the cush I smoked with Trina hadn't completely worn off yet. No wonder he'd been pulling my strings all this time. It felt good watching him squirm. I bunned my hair and stepped into the shower. I could see him stewing through the glass.

"Fatima. We're gonna talk. I'm not letting you get away with disappearing on me. So do you want to do it, now or later?" He folded his arms and waited. Ignoring him I continued to wash up. I still didn't have anything to say. If he thought I'd be bending to his will, he had another thing coming. If anyone should be answering questions, it was his ass, not me. While washing my hair, I reached behind me and blindly searched for my shampoo bar. Instead, I found his chest. I could recognize every rip and cut on his body, with or without my vision. I probably knew his body better than my own.

"What are you doing in here?" I asked, slightly annoyed.

I knew, he didn't think he was getting any. Not after what I found out. As much as, I wanted him to leave. I still didn't feel like arguing. So I pretended he wasn't there. Darius wasn't the man I thought he was, but I couldn't help still loving him. When he scooped me into his strong arms earlier, it took everything I had inside of me not to melt. Even though, my dream of being his wife, and mother of his children was permanently put on the back burner. I wasn't ready to let him go. Not yet anyway. I tried to get him out of my system by reliving my college days with Shana and Denise. But it didn't work. I still thought about him the entire time I was gone. None of the men that approached me came closing to getting my attention.

"What? You didn't miss this when you were gone?" He said, stepping close behind me as he slid his dick along my lips below.

Instantly, my mind started thinking nothing and everything at the same time. What was he doing? Wasn't he just in the middle of bitching me out. Now all of sudden he wants to fuck? I wasn't prepared for this. I expected him to cuss me out or want to fight, but not this. What was he thinking?

Darius started teasing me by rocking back and forth without taking the plunge. Then he grabbed more than a handful of my breast and squeezed, before twisting and flicking my nipples which was driving me wild. The warm stream of the shower fell between us, and only heightened my excitement. Every part of my mind, said get out! Run away. Danger. Danger. It's not safe here. But, my legs wouldn't move. I was just a helpless victim to the hold he had over me. It was feeling too damn good stop now.

His wet lips landed on the curve of my neck as he peeked his manhood in and out of my honey pot. She was hot, wet, and ready to play. I couldn't help wrapping my legs around his waist. He grabbed my cheeks and beat it up until, I was screaming his name, not caring who heard the pleasure I was in. Damn. I loved being teased. And he knew it.

Just before I was ready to cum, he pulled out and spun me around. My hands slapped against the marble shower wall, before he entered me from behind.

"Do you like that?" He asked through clenched teeth.

"Yes. Daddy. Give to me. It feels so good." I screamed back at him." Pumping away, he said, "Good. I'm glad I've got your attention." Darius pulled out and slammed his nine inch dick into my ass. The pain was so great, I tried to drop to my knees but he wouldn't let me.

"Don't move." He said, while grabbing my throat and thrusting away.

"You brought this on yourself. All you had to do was listen. But you couldn't do that. Instead you wanted to leave and act like a stupid bitch. So now you have to be punished."

He hammered against my body, not caring that he was tearing me apart. My head felt light and dizzy, while every muscle in my body tingled and ached. I wailed for him to stop, but he just went harder. It was like my pain turned him on. Finally, he grunted in relief, before pulling out and allowing me to collapse onto the concrete floor.

"Don't you ever think about leaving again. If you try, I'll kill you. Now get yourself together. That little stunt you pulled put us behind schedule. You still have to get my money. So be ready to meet my brother tomorrow. I've got everything setup." He turned to leave, but then I saw his feet pivot in my direction.

"And if you think I'm playing, try me. I love you Fatima. I really do. But if you betray me again, I'll make this feel like a dream compared to what I'll do to you next." He stepped out of the shower, and left me to cry on the floor. The taste of salt filled my mouth as I balled up on the floor. I couldn't lift my head, let alone my body. I had no energy left. I watched the blood stained water run down the drain, in disbelief. How could I have been so stupid?

Chapter Ten

I hadn't spoken to anyone since what happened last night. What could I say? And to who? There wasn't anyone who gave a fuck about me to call. I couldn't call Tasha. That relationship was trash, since I found out she had a child with Darius. Actually, it was shit much earlier than that. I was just too stupid to realize it. Besides, our chances of savaging any possible friendship died, when I jumped her with Trina and the girls. And I honestly can't say I regret it. I could never look at her the same.

After Darius was done, he left for a few hours. There was no conversation or exchange between us, which I have to say I appreciated. I couldn't handle looking into the void, he called eyes. I still couldn't. It was too much. I knew, I was partially responsible for what happened. He obviously was concerned about where I had been, and instead of telling him, or responding directly, I played games like a child. I should have simply respected his feelings, and cooperated when he requested to talk. But like an idiot, I didn't. So I paid the consequences.

When he came back to my apartment last night, he pulled me into his arms after coming to bed, and kissed me good night. My heart nearly flipped over and out of my chest, when he touched me. Every part of me wanted to jump out of bed screaming.

But I knew better. It would only make matters worse. I fell into a twilight sleep for a few hours, but still had so many questions running through my mind at the same time. Mainly, how could he do what he did to me? I knew he had issues, of course. But I never thought he could hurt me so badly. I truly believed he loved me. Maybe not in the traditional sense, but in his own way. Now I realize, he couldn't possibly care about me, or anyone else. There is no denying, Darius was a devil in men's clothing. The physical pain he put me through was nothing compared to the emotional rot he left in the center of my chest. He knew what I went through growing up in the system, and promised to never hurt me like that. In fact, he swore I'd never go through anything remotely similar to what I experienced in foster care, as long as I stayed by his side. Only to turn around and do the same thing he swore to protect me against. How could he?

"Fatima. You ready?" He asked breaking my thoughts.

"Yeah." I said, staring out the car window, avoiding his eyes.

Darius sat in the drivers side of my black Toyota Camry. He hadn't said much all morning. However he did, pick out my clothes for the day which was a short sundress, a half jean jacket, and pair of brown wedge heels. I didn't care for the combo, but didn't protest. The funny thing was he also made breakfast, and even ran my bath water, as if it would change what he did to me. The drive over to the hospital was quiet, until now. I was looking forward to getting away from him for a few moments. Even though, the last time I was here, I saw him and Tasha together through the emergency room window.

"I know things have been rough for you lately. But I don't want you to give up on us. Couples go through rough patches. This is just one of them." He couldn't have said what I think he said. Could he? A rough patch. That's what he called raping his own fiance. I turned my hips away from him and clung to the passenger side door. This monster wasn't worth talking too. Especially since, nothing I said or felt mattered to him anyway.

"Fatima. I love you. I just needed to make you understand what you did wasn't okay. You get that now right?" His large hand palmed my knee, while I mentally kicked him off of me.

"I know baby. I love you too," seemed like the only way to respond. He proved to me he was limitless. I saw the real him last night. There was no way, I could ever forget who I was dealing with. I sure wasn't going test my chances. I knew I was treading dangerous waters.

"That's my girl … Now go over the game plan we discussed. We can't mess this up. If were still going to get married and have a little baby running around soon." My stomach twisted at the thought of the idea. A baby with him, was the last thing I wanted. I'd get an abortion first.

"Tasha is going to bring DeMarcus. So I can take him to his checkup with your brother. I'm supposed to tell him, Tasha couldn't get off work to take him to his appointment, which is why I'm doing it for her. Then, you want me to ask him out. So I can get closer to him in order to steal his financial information for you." I watched as a happy couple came out of the hospital with their new bundle of joy. Just a few weeks ago, I thought we'd be them soon. Now, I wished we never met.

"I need you to steal his information. So we can have the life we want. This isn't just for me. It's for us. Remember that. This is a team effort okay? Everyone has to play their part." He said, pulling my chin to face him.

"Okay." I agreed, wanting to be anywhere but with him.

"By the way, I know what you did the other night."

"What do you mean?" I asked, trying to figure what trick he was going to pull out his hat next.

"I went to see Tasha the other day, and she was all lumped up. She said it was you and a few other bitches. At first I thought she had to be confused. It couldn't have been you. Like a fool, I defended you to her. Then I saw how you where behaving when you came home, and realized she was telling me the truth."

I could feel a migraine coming on. That bitch never stopped being a pain in my ass. She knew she deserved that ass whopping. It was the only justice I got out of the whole situation. Still, I didn't want to get on his bad side. There was no telling what he would do to me, if I did. I tried to explain.

"Darius I …" I began to speak, but he cut me off.

"You don't have to explain. I know why you did it. Hell, I'd fuck somebody up if they ever laid a finger on you. Outside of this situation, of course. As sad as the circumstances are right now, I understand you may have to give my brother a little pussy in order to keep my black ass out of jail. Even though I understand where you're coming from, I can't have you hitting the mother of my child again. You're my future wife and everything, but I can't have you two fighting. Y'all are going to have to work together. Because if you think about it, technically, the two of you are like family."

He had every fluid in my body boiling. Like family? Me and that bitch were already like family, before his dick got in the way. I couldn't believe what he was saying. I just wanted to get the hell away from him.

"Do you hear me?" He asked, irritated.

"I hear you. It won't happen again."

Tasha pulled up in her beat up Honda Civic just in time, because I was too through with his conversation. Little DeMarcus was looking good from what I could see, but he did have a sling on his arm. We all stepped out and gathered in the parking lot.

"Aunty Fatty." DeMarcus called, running to me with a huge smile on his face.

"Hi baby." I cooed back, I was just as excited to see him. I swept him up while avoiding his arm. Then waited for Darius' instructions.

"Tasha." he probed.

"Hey Fatima." She said sucking her teeth, and rolling her eyes.

"Hey." I said, smirking at her. We really fucked her up. Her left eye was the exact opposite of her high yellow complexion. It looked like a lumpy plum sitting on top of her face. She had random scratches and bruises everywhere from what I could see. I had to admit, I enjoyed seeing her look how I felt.

"I don't want no funny business going on with

my baby." She put her hand on her hip, and positioned herself in front of me. The bitch was trying to intimidate me. Apparently, she wanted more of the other night.

"Cut that shit out." Darius reprimanded her, before I could respond. She knew better than to think I would hurt a child. Even though, I had been acting out of character lately, that part of me would never change.

"You know Fatima loves those kids. I won't let you keep mine or the other two away from her. Y'all are going to learn to love each other, again. This shit is exactly why, I kept everything sealed up. You two are both too selfish to see the big picture."

I ignored them both and played with baby. This nigga was crazy, and Tasha was a basic bitch. So I didn't have anything to contribute to the conversation.

"We'll be back in about an hour. Text me when you're done." He said, pecking me on the lips., They both took off in separate cars.

It felt like we were in the waiting room forever. DeMarcus had fallen asleep ten minutes ago, and my arm was already completely numb. He was a big boy for four years old.

"DeMarcus Stewart."

"Finally."

I gathered my purse before heading to the back. She took his weight, height, and temperature. Then lead us to the examination room where I started sweating bullets. I hadn't dated or thought about a man in three years. Now Darius expected me to seduce one. That was his brother no less. I didn't even know where to start.

"Good Afternoon. Ms. Stewart. I'm Dr. Du Bois. Nice to meet you." His massive hand swallowed my slim fingers. His presence and frame was larger than life, but he had a gentle aura, I couldn't quite place. He began looking over his chart while I rocked DeMarcus back and forth.

While he was reading I couldn't help noticing, he was even better looking than Darius which was really saying something. His skin was rich and dark like the finest marble money could buy. When he smiled his skin and teeth competed to out shine each other, but neither could win. There was no way to pick between them. They were both so beautiful. I was sitting down when he came into the room. But it appeared he was a good three inches taller than Darius, which was an added bonus for an Amazon like me. I had to admit, he was impressive. A tall, dark, and handsome single black doctor was hard to find. Too bad I met his psychotic brother first.

"Ms. Stewart. Are you alright?" He said, waving his hands in front of my face.

"Uh. Yes. I'm sorry … I'm fine." I stammered. "Just a little tired. I'm Ms. Butler by the way. His mother couldn't take off work. So, I brought him instead."

He must have been trying to talk to me the entire time I was ogling his goodies. My throat dried out from embarrassment. I definitely wasn't getting off on a good foot. Marcus asked standard medical questions about his health, and checked his arm. When he examined DeMarcus he was so sweet and lighthearted. He made jokes and gave him a sucker. DeMarcus was immediately asking when he could come back to the doctor again. If that wasn't a sign he knew how to do his job well, I didn't know what was. Watching him, stirred up feelings of regret. I missed my job as a teacher. Even though, it was summer time. I knew I had no job to return when the school year started again. Thinking over the last few weeks, it hit me how much Eddie threatening to squeal ruined my life. Things weren't ever the same after Darius found out.

"Well. It looks like everything is okay. Stacy will setup your next appointment at the front desk." He smiled and motioned towards the door." Shit. I got lost in him, I totally forgot why the hell I was even here.

"Dr. Du Bois." I rushed behind him, unsure of what to say. " Excuse me. I was wondering. Is there a Mrs. Du Bois?" I asked, nervously.

He flashed that handsome of smile of his, and grabbed his chin. At the very least he was flattered by question. "No. It's just me."

"I hate to take up your time. I know you're a busy man." Before I could finish, he put up his hand to stop me.

"Ms. Butler, you really are a beautiful woman. Any man would be lucky to have you. I'm just not in the market right now. But thanks." He gave me a weak smile, then left. Damn. What was I going to do.

Chapter Eleven

As expected, Darius acted like a caged animal when I told him Marcus turned me down. He flipped practically every surface over in the house during his rage. No matter how many different ways I tried to explain he wasn't interested. He kept giving me the same answer. Figure it out. There was only a week left, before Eddie's arraignment. Which meant time was running out fast. It was obvious he was feeling the fire, and as a result, so was I. There had to be a way for me to get close to Marcus. After spending several hours trying to come up with different ways to bump into him, I finally discovered a practical solution. I would literally have to be a little more reckless in my approach.

I pulled into the parking space across from Marcus's vehicle. Perfect. He hadn't left for work yet. Killing time, I grabbed my rear view mirror and double checked my makeup. My lips could definitely use another coat of my favorite red lipstick, Rubywoo. It was like confidence in a tube. I could never go wrong when swiping it on. It was the perfect compliment to my smooth honey complexion.

As I waited, I thought about our visit the other day. Surprisingly, I hadn't stopped thinking about him since. There was something so sweet and mysterious in his eyes. Even though, he smiled and put on a good face, I could tell there was pain underneath it. When I was around him, I felt like we were kindred spirits. He was so tender and patient with DeMarcus. It was refreshing to see a man be so gentle. Being around him stirred something up in my spirit that I can't quite put my finger on. It never occurred to me there might actually be benefits to meeting him. I had dreaded the this day for so long. Especially since Darius wanted me to con him. At first I rejected the idea because I didn't want to be romantic with another man. Now, I didn't want to because Marcus didn't deserve to be another one of Darius's victims. Of course, I wanted to avoid the wrath of Darius at all cost, but spending time with Marcus was no punishment. I just hated the fact, he was a pawn in a sick game.

From the corner of my eye, I could see Marcus leaving the hospital main entrance. I pushed up my girls, nested in my yellow form fitted dress, and prepared to put on my best performance. Backing up, I slammed into the back of his Nissan Altma. The tail light and fender were hanging off, now.

"Hey! Watch where the hell you're going." He shouted, waving arms above his head.

I jumped out of the car, and mocked innocence. "Oh my god. I'm so sorry. I didn't realize how close you were. Can you forgive me?" I inspected the damage I caused accidentally on purpose, while he stood by steaming.

"How the hell couldn't you have seen my vehicle? There's no traffic. It obviously wasn't going anywhere." He was pissed, and not taking the fender bender as well as I hoped.

"Please forgive me. Wait here. I'll give you my policy information." I ran to my car and grabbed want I needed from out the glove box. I checked my side mirror to see if he was watching and he wasn't. This guy wasn't going to be easy to break.

"Here you go." I said, passing my info over.

"Thanks." Marcus headed to his car to leave.

"Wait up." I ran to his side, before he could sit down in the drivers seat. "I was hoping, I could take you out to make up, for my little accident." I said, giving him my sweetest smile.

"Is that what this is about." He said, crossing his arms. "I told you the other day, I wasn't interested. Just let up. Okay."

His tone wasn't mean, but it certainly was final. I had to go home, and tell Darius, I failed. There was no telling what he was going to do to me. All of sudden, I saw myself crying on the shower floor as my blood circled down the drain. The memory sent me into a panic, my heart sank to the pit of my stomach, and I began to cry.

"Hey. Don't do that. Okay. I'm sorry." He said, wrapping his arms around me.

I cried into his chest knowing, tonight would be an encore of what happened the other night. There was no way around it. Darius made it clear, he needed the money to stay out of jail, and I owed him for everything he gave me. One way or anther, I was going to have to pay him back. Marcus rubbed my back until I stopped sobbing into his chest. I'm sure he thought I was crazy now. If he didn't before. The front of his white coat was soaked in my tears, and smeared with makeup, but he didn't seem to mind. He wiped the back of his hand across my cheeks, and gave me a weak smile. I couldn't understand why this man, I was trying to con was being so sweet to me after I intentionally wrecked his car. Deep inside, I knew I didn't deserve his kindness or concern. But it still felt good nonetheless.

"Thank you. I'm such a mess." I said, feeling a mixture of guilt and shame.

"Don't worry about. Are you okay?" His eyes were filled with genuine concerned, which only made me feel worse. I didn't want to do anything to cause this man anymore trouble. I surely didn't want to help Darius. He was a monster, but I knew not doing what he said, only meant more pain and misery for me.

"Yeah. I really am sorry about your car. I'd really like to make it up to you by taking you out to eat." I'm sure I looked as pathetic as I felt. But I had to give it one last shot, before going home.

At first Marcus didn't respond. He just gave me a sympathetic smile. I'm sure the poor guy didn't know what the hell to say. I started to turn towards my vehicle, but he stopped me.

"Saying no to a beautiful woman is hard. But saying no to a beautiful woman in tears is impossible. I'll go, but I can't let you pay. I'll pick you up tomorrow night. Just text me your contact information." He said handing me a card.

I couldn't believe it. He actually agreed, after seeing me wail like an unstable idiot. I wanted to faint, skip, and cry all at the same time. Thank god he agreed to meet me.

*****

We'd been sitting across from each other for at least thirty minutes, but not much was said. My fear was becoming a reality. Marcus agreed to come out with me, but it was clear he wasn't ecstatic. For what reason, I didn't know. I never had a problem attracting men before, but he seemed really uninterested.

"So what made you decide to become a doctor?" I asked trying to stir up conversation.

"Do you want to know the truth, because it's pretty depressing."

I couldn't possibly imagine anything more depressing than sitting here another minute with him in silence. So his question was pretty easy to answer.

"Of course I want to know the truth. It can't be much worse than some of the things I've been through."

"Well. When I was growing up. I had a little brother, Eric. He was a tough little guy. And pain in my ass. But I loved him." Marcus shook his head and stared at his plate. It was obvious he was strolling down memory lane.

"Anyway. He got mangled up pretty bad by a train. I really don't care to get into the details, but I knew I wanted to help kids feel better, after what happened to him."

Looking across the table, I could see sincere pain in his eyes. I hated bringing up unwanted memories. Especially, since Darius already told me about their brother. There was no point, in making him recall such a miserable childhood event. The night was definitely going down hill fast, I had never been on such an awkward date in my life. I desperately needed a drink.

"I don't get out very often. I take it you don't either?" I said trying to lighten the mood.

"Oh can you tell." he said, laughing.

"The last time I went on a date was before my wife died."

He didn't again. The heavy blows just kept on coming. I knew something good must have happened in his life.

"I'm sorry to hear that. What happened?" I really didn't want to hear anything negative, but I'd choose bad conversation over no conversation any day.

"She had just left the school with our daughter, and some careless asshole decided to get on the road drunk. Man. I can't believe that was over three years ago." He shook his head and wore the same expression he did when talking about his brother, before waving down the waitress.

"Can I get a shot of tequila? And whatever the lady wants." He ordered.

"I'll take the same." I was happy to see we were finally on the same page. The waitress brought us our drinks, and we started knocking shots back, one after another, until we were lose enough to speak freely.

"So Marcus?" I said, leaning on the table with my arms pressed against my breasts. "Am I your type?" I genuinely wanted to know, because even though conversation had picked up. He still hadn't made any plays.

He laughed and took another shot. "I don't have a type."

"Bullshit. Everyone has a type. What did your wife look like?"

The smile was wiped clean off his face. It was obvious I caught him off guard.

"You don't have to answer that, if you don't want." I said, trying to clean up the mess I made.

"No. You didn't say anything wrong. She was petite, and blonde."

"Oh." I said, laughing. "That explains a lot."

"What does that mean?"

"It means. You were never interested me, because I'm a black girl. Light, but still black. Not to mention the fact, that I'm tall." Marcus licked his lips and eyed me from head to toe from across the table.

"There's absolutely nothing, I don't find attractive about you. Like I said. I don't have a type. I'm into the whole woman. Not just spare parts."

"Is that right." He certainly piqued my interest. I

wanted to know everything about this mysterious man who healed sick children, survived losing his family, and still managed to be decent.

"Would either of you like another drink?" The waitress asked. Marcus shook his head no. I on the other hand, asked for two additional shots. I was going to have to be loaded in order to screw him over, literally and figuratively.

"Maybe, you should take it easy."

Marcus reached across the table and squeezed my hand. It was clearly his attempt to enhance his words. But what he said didn't matter, because I had already decided to get annihilated before leaving the house. How was I going to steal from this kindhearted person? I already felt bad about what Darius asked me to do, before finding out his wife and child died. He already had so much tragedy in his life. I didn't want to be the reason for anymore.

"When was the last time you made love to a woman, Marcus?" I asked in a sultry voice. I knew, asking him about sex would change the subject. No man could resist listening to his little head. Not even the good doctor.

Marcus cleared his throat, pulled at his collar, and began to sweat. Apparently, it had been quite sometime. "You get right down to business, don't you?" He said, looking around nervously.

I wanted him to take me home. As sad as the situation was I really liked being with him. Maybe it was naive or reckless for me to think we could be together, but I really wanted to see where things could go. Darius had no plans on setting me free. I knew if I helped him stay out of jail, I'd be imprisoning myself. Attaching myself to Marcus was my best bet. If anyone could protect me against Darius, it would be Marcus. He had to know him better than anyone else, which is why I decided to get as drunk as humanly possible. He'd have to take me home then. It was the easiest way to avoid going home to Darius.

Chapter Twelve

After our schizophrenic date, Marcus carried me up the stairs and into his cottage style bedroom. He was the perfect gentleman. When I woke up, I saw him reading in a lazy boy recliner across the room. I looked down and realized I had the same clothes on from the night before. My purse and shoes were stacked neatly on top of the wooden chest in front of his bed. To my surprise, he didn't try to undress or make a pass at me. It was strange and unusual to feel so safe with someone I just met. He smiled and continued reading when he saw I was awake. When I thought about how drunk I got, I started to feel self conscious and insecure. Maybe he took pity on me, and that's why he let me stay. If he felt that way, he didn't show it. In fact, Marcus treated me like a welcomed quest. The entire time we spent together, I found no judgment in his eyes or voice. There was no way he could have been more chill about the situation.

At first, the vibe in his home threw me off. There was no traffic or loud voices outside the walls. Instead, I heard birds, insects, and wild life from his bedroom window. It was strange and amazing. I didn't know where I was, and honestly didn't care. I was just happy to be far from home. He lived miles away from the city, which allowed me to imagine I was a different person living under new circumstances. All Fourth of July weekend – we ate, read, and made love like we knew each other for years. He was so relaxed and out of practice, he allowed me to take control of the wheel, which I desperately needed after my horrible experience with Darius. I have to admit the last couple of days with him read like a passage straight out of a romance novel. If I didn't have a small bomb ticking in the back of my head. I would have thought I died, and woke up in heaven.

I rolled over and smiled at Marcus sleeping beside me. He single-handedly restored my faith in love and life in a matter of days. Who knew, we'd fall for each other so hard. Especially since, I had to beg before he would come out with me. As I watched him sleep a tinge of guilt overwhelmed me. This wonderful man revealed everything to me. Meanwhile I was keeping secrets that could hurt us both.

"Good morning, beautiful." He said, propping up on his elbow while giving me a crooked smile. "How'd you sleep?"

"Better than ever." I replied, placing a soft kiss on his lips. As cheesy as it may sound, I was telling the truth. I've never slept so well in my life. Out here in the boonies life was simple. We were able to spend the entire three day weekend enjoying each other. Since his practice was closed due to the holiday.

"You know today's the Fourth, right? What do you want to do?" I asked, knowing tomorrow was Eddie's arraignment. I had no desire to go anywhere. Because I didn't want to risk bumping into Darius.

"I'm good with staying home. I really don't like the city life. I'd rather spend more time at home with you."

Buzz Buzz Buzz

My cell phone started vibrating on the bed. How the hell did I forget to put it back in my purse? I must have gotten lost in the moment last night. Marcus reached for my phone, before I could. Panicking, I snatched it out of his hand.

"Jesus." He yelled, yanking his hand away from me.

"I'm sorry baby. Let me see." Dammit. I didn't mean to hurt him. Darius had been blowing my phone up since our date the other night. He kept sending me messages every few minutes. I read none of them, because I wasn't going home no matter what they said. Marcus was being so good to me. I hated not being able to tell him the truth. But I didn't know how to explain the situation yet. I needed a little more time. So I avoided the subject all together.

I ran to the bathroom, and got a wash cloth to cover his cut. Unfortunately, I got him pretty good. I dabbed at the broken skin on his hand, even though it wasn't bleeding.

"Fatima. I'm fine. It's nothing. Trust me. I'm a doctor remember."

"I know. I'm just sorry I hurt you, babe." I said pouting.

Sitting on the bed across from each other, I could tell there was something he wanted to say by the way he was studying me. If I wasn't so afraid a bone would fall out of my mouth, I would have asked what was wrong.

"Is there something you want to tell me?"

"No. I don't think so. Should there be?" I feigned innocence and hoped for the best.

"I admit. I've been out of the game along time, but I'm not an idiot."

Dammit. He wasn't going to let up.

"Who was calling your phone? Your husband, boyfriend, friend with benefits? Who?" He looked concerned and a little hurt. I didn't know what to say to relieve his stress. Telling him the truth wasn't going to do it. It would only stress us both out more.

"No. I'm not with anyone but you. Some idiot

keeps calling to speak to Angie. I've told him hundred times, this is not Angie's phone. But he keeps calling."

It was obvious he didn't believe me, but thankfully he let the conversation go. I was off the hook. At least for the moment.

*****

Marcus was in the kitchen cooking up some catfish he caught earlier today. While I went to check the weather on the nightly news in the living room. We had old school rhythm and blues playing in the background, and the entire front room lit up with vanilla scented candles. Sitting in front of the television with a flute of red wine in hand, I could tell tonight was going to be good.

The usual boring stories about politics, sports, and new developments came on before they got to weather. "It looks like tomorrow is going to be a good day for fishing. It's supposed to rain." I yelled back towards the kitchen.

"Thanks babe."

I got up to join Marcus in the kitchen, but the next report got my attention.

"There was a fire located at 555 Parkway

Avenue in the Greenwood Park Addition. Authorities can't say for certain who was caught in the fire. But they suspect the only tenant living there by the name of Darius Du Bois was the unidentified body found badly burned …" The reported continued, but I couldn't hear a word she said. That monster found away to escape the system.

"What's wrong? Is everything okay?" Marcus was cleaning up the broken wine glass, I apparently dropped on his maple hardwood floor. I didn't even realize it fell. While he was knelt down in front of the television, I could see he began to listen to the report.

"Hell yeah." He cheered. Karma finally got that bastard. How about another drink? My night just got a whole lot better?" He asked before jogging to the kitchen to get two wine glasses.

Was he actually happy his brother was dead? I felt like I had deja vu. Darius responded the same way after finding out his father was died.

"Here," he said, thrusting a glass of wine in my hand. "Oh, don't look at me like that. That monster was related to me by chromosomes only. You'd understand if you knew what he was capable of." Marcus clinked his glass against mine and took a big swallow. "Thank you Jesus." He said, before running to check on our dinner.

Of course, I knew exactly what Darius was capable of. Or at least I thought I did. What possibly could have happened to make them hate each other so much. According to Darius, he ran away from home after Eric's death, and never saw Marcus again. I had to find out what was going on.

"Bottoms up." I said, joining him in the kitchen. I drank the rest of my wine, and hopped on the counter. "Do you want to share why we're celebrating your brother's death? It's kind of creepy. Don't you agree?"

Marcus rubbed his hands together, then gripped my knee caps. He was clearly excited to share the good news.

"I refuse to admit any relation to it. I can't even standing talking about it. You remember the reason I became a doctor, right?"

"Of course. Your little brother, Eric got hit by a train. So you decided to become a pediatrician."

"That's only part of the story. My brother didn't just get hit by a train. It took him out in the middle of the night, and tied him to the railings. By the time, neighborhood kids found his body it was nothing but cracked bones, torn tendons, and rotten flesh. The bastard came home and slept like a baby. Knowing exactly what he did to my brother. My family never recovered. Both my parents became alcoholics. They stayed together until my dad died.

101

But they were both like the walking dead after it happened. Things were never the same. The only reason we discovered what it did was because the rope wrapped around Eric's rib cage was still there. That's why I'm glad the motherfucker burned to death."

Marcus looked overjoyed. He wasn't hiding enthusiasm over Darius's mock death. How could I tell him, there wasn't anything to celebrate because the monster was still alive. Feeling sick I excused myself to the bathroom. I had to figure out a way to tell him the truth. Now that Darius was practically the invisible man. There was no doubt in my mind, he'd come after us.

All of a sudden the lights went out in the bathroom. I flipped the switch up and down, but they wouldn't come back on. Out of now where, there was a loud thud and crashing sound from downstairs. I tripped over my feet scrambling to place my ear against the door. Silence. Should I peak my head into the hallway to see what was going on? Maybe he fell or knocked over the television, because he wasn't paying attention. No. He would at least yell, he was okay, right? Suddenly, my phone began to ring. A familiar sinking feeling enveloped my body. Please don't let it be him. This time I checked my phone to see who was calling, 156 unread text messages, flashed across the screen. I opened the newest one and saw it was Darius. See you soon was all it read.

Chapter Thirteen

I traveled further down the blacked out hallway upstairs with my back firmly pressed against the wall. I thought about all possible options, and scenarios. It was possible the power went out naturally for some unforeseen reason. Darius could have nothing to do with it, the loud crash coming from downstairs, or my phone suddenly being out of service. But the chances were slim. Hell. Who was I kidding? The chances weren't slim. The small bumps running over my entire body confirmed what I already knew. He found me.

The floor creaked as I slowly placed my feet against the hardwood floor. Turning the corner, I saw Marcus's bedroom door was open. I'd have to take my chances scaling down the old wood framed window. Reaching the doorway, I saw no one was there. I hurried inside, unlatched the window, and threw my legs over the edge. Looking down, I could see a line of small scrubs beneath my dangling feet. Maybe they'd soften the fall. It was a risk because Marcus parked his car close to the bushes. So things could go bad, or really really bad. I let out a heavy sigh, closed my eyes, and jumped.

AAH!

By the time I realized he was there, my head

snapped back, my body followed, and he was dragging back inside. How the hell did he know I was here? He must have been watching me the entire time. I screamed for help, but the dirt country road stayed quiet and empty. No one turned on a light or pulled back their curtains. It was just the two of us, fighting alone in the darkness. Where was Marcus? Did he kill him? I thrashed at his hands, and bucked like a thoroughbred. There was no doubt, I was fighting for my life. Still, he wouldn't let go.

A raised nail ripped through my calf as he yanked me through the rustic bedroom window. Blood soaked the bottom of my pants as I twisted and bucked, trying to break free. But he was a powerhouse with shoulders as wide as a refrigerator. His towering build was as strong, and stout as any linebacker. Unfortunately, he was aimed at me. I was no match for him. Still, I gave it my all, but it was no use … he had me.

On the way in, the sound of spilled furniture filled the room. Disheveled, I searched for my phone, unable to see anything. I completely forgot it was out of service. My head was so dizzy, and spun out of control, I didn't even realize my mistake. The back of my neck ached, and my scalp felt like it was on fire. I stammered to my feet trying to get his massive hands unlocked from my hair.

"Get the fuck off of me," I roared. I wasn't going to make it easy for him to take me out. This was a kill he'd have to earn. I wasn't some naive and defenseless little boy like his brother..

Darius laughed as he drug me around the dark room. "Look at you," he jived. "I told you, I'd find you. You'll never be free, unless I say so." He kneed me in the back and let go of my hair.

Palming the old wood floor, I saved my face from smacking against it. Propping up on my hands and knees, I crawled around the room searching for the door. The sound of my breathe and thudding heart was so loud, it was difficult to hear, where he was in the room. But the raised hairs on the back of my neck told me he wasn't far away.

You thought you could out smart me?" he growled from across the room. "They can't catch me. I'm the living dead." He cackled. "It's just you and me baby, like the good old days."

His feet raced across the room, just as soon as I found the door. Eagerly I turned the nob and pushed. It was just short of completely opening, but then it slammed back close. "What the fuck?" I screamed. I stood on my knees and reached above my head. Dammit. The chain was latched.

Darius grabbed me by my waist and threw me across the room. My back arched in pain. How could he see me? There wasn't a hint of light anywhere. "You remember my promise don't you?" His stride sent vibrations through the floor board which gave me a general idea of his direction. Using the back of my elbows, I quietly squirmed away from him. If memory served me right, I was only a few feet from the window directly beside the bed. Jumping out of it, was my only viable option.

"Where you going, huh?" He said, pulling me up by the neck of my shirt. "I thought I told you Fatty, it's me and you till the end." Darius threw me on the bed, grabbed my throat, and pulled down my pants. He was going to rape. I swung at his face and neck, but it didn't deter him. My hands were met with something solid and hard, that wasn't his face. Heavy droplets fell onto my forehead. I thought it was his sweat, but soon realized it was my own blood falling from my knuckles.

"Yeah. That's my girl." He said, moaning in pleasure. Despite my best efforts I lost. He was already deep inside me. I wailed for him to stop, but he just kept going. Exhausted and weak, I quit fighting. I couldn't say how long it lasted. My mind took me to another place. I just starred into the darkness around me and left.

RAH AAH!

The sound of man howling, jarred me out of my trance. Suddenly, I realized he wasn't on top of me anymore, and I sat up. It was daybreak. The weak

107

light of the early morning sun crept into the room, just in time for me to see Marcus charging towards him. Darius was standing next to the bed dressed like a special ops solider. I looked down at my broken knuckles covered in blood, and quickly realized I was hammering my fists against the night vision mask he had covering his face. Caught off guard, Marcus sent him careening out the bedroom window. I jumped out of bed, and ran towards Marcus. I wanted to make sure he was okay. There was a tourniquet wrapped tightly around his neck, and both of his eyes were swelled shut. There was no question, he gave Darius a good fight. He knuckles were swollen and busted like he'd been beating a brick wall. We both limped to the window and looked outside, but Darius was no where in sight. Marcus immediately bolted downstairs hot on his trail. In horror, I dropped to my knees, and wailed in disbelief. I couldn't believe he got away.

TORN BETWEEN TWO BROTHERS

VOLUME II

Chapter 1

Darius

"Fuck!" I roared into the exhaust filled sky. Eddie blackmailed me, after everything I did for his punk ass. My business paid for his house, his car, his wife, and his bitch. Plus all his kids, known and unknown, and the muthafucker still turned his back on me. My life wouldn't be a mess right now, if he stuck to the plan. It didn't even matter though, everything was already done.

Stealing papers wasn't as easy as it sounded. The cash came so fast, it had me thinking I was invincible, and completely off the radar. In a lot of ways, white collar crime was higher risk than hustling on the street. Even the best operation was like a house of cards. One wrong move, and the house came falling down.

I thought, I had the perfect business plan. Eddie stole the facts. Tool opened the credit accounts. And I pulled the strings from behind the scene, of course. When things went sour, I had to think fast. Eddie wasn't cooperating. Tool was clueless. And my Pops failed me in the end. I was really counting on that life insurance money, too. Too bad he fucked me over, even in death. I couldn't believe

111

the muthafucker had the audacity to leave me a bible. If he wasn't already dead, I would've killed his ass for disrespecting me like that, and in front of a lawyer no less. Just thinking about that shit, pissed me off. I had a reputation to protect.

Unfortunately, circumstances forced my hand, literally and figuratively. In one full swoop, Tool used a red hot blade to chop it off. I was so spun, and out of my mind, I took the blade from his ass, and sliced his head off. Taking Tool out wasn't originally apart of my plan. Getting fucked up on bath salts was supposed to help me man up. So he could do his business, without me punking out. He warned me against taking that shit. But I needed something to fuck my mind up. Otherwise, I couldn't go through with it. Coke and Crystal had been good to me in the past. But, they didn't have the edge I needed go through with it. So I took the bath salts, anyway.

My house was supposed to burn to the ground with my hand inside. It was supposed to be the evidence of my death. Now that I thought about it, the original plan was stupid, and faulty as fuck. I needed a body. Thank god, Tool and I had the same build. It was his body burning up in flames, not mine. I made sure to set him aflame first. Most of his body was ash by the time I threw my hand in the fire. Everything worked out better than I planned. Damn, I could be so resourceful. I couldn't help patting myself on the back. Talk about turning lemons into lemonade. It may sound extreme, but now I was free to do whatever I wanted, without worrying about getting caught. I still had unfinished business with Eddie though. He destroyed my relationship, house, and killed my best friend, Tool. I'd have to deal with his punk ass later. Right now, none of that mattered. I had more important things to attend to like Fatima and Darius.

I didn't understand how everything went so wrong. All I needed was her cooperation. And we'd be living large right now. She'd have the house, baby, and marriage she always wanted. If she could have just held on for a little bit longer. But no. The bitch couldn't hang. On second thought, let me take that back. Fatima wasn't a bitch. She was special. I knew she wasn't cut out for the job, but I tried to bring her along, anyway. I should of asked that bitch Tasha to put in the work. She would have fucked my brother and stole his money, without a second thought. She maybe a low budget bitch, but she was a top notch ho. I had to plan better next time.

I thought Fatima could help me stay out of jail by conning my brother. The bitch hadn't got any pussy since his wife and kid died. It should have been an easy job. Looking back, I realize I was selfish, because Fatima was too delicate for a nigga like me. She was a fucking school teacher for goodness sake. I loved her so much, because she gave me a chance, anyway. Unlike everyone else in my life, she didn't judge me according to my past. I lied in the beginning of our relationship about my job, but when she found out, she stayed. When I told her about what happened to Eddie, I knew she'd leave me. But to my surprise, she didn't.

It was true, I left out the fact, I tied him to the railroad tracks. I just wanted to see what would happen. It was innocent child's play. He begged and cried. He even pissed his pants. I tried my best not to laugh, but I couldn't help it. Watching him plead for his life made me fell like a god. I got lost in the thrill, and forgot about my plan to untie him, before the train came. It really was my intention to set him free, but his cries were like cake. I couldn't eat enough. By the time, I snapped out of my trance, the train already got him. I felt bad. But what could I do. The damage was literally already done. So I walked home, and went to bed.

I trudged down the shoulder of the highway while people stuck their heads out the window laughing, cat calling, and telling me to get dressed. I had on a wife beater, pair of Calvin Klein boxer briefs, and a pair of combat boots. I had to ditch all my high tech gear after that bitch sent me flying out the window. Man I hated his guts. Ever since he were kids, Marcus was outshining or destroying my plans. Everybody preferred him. My mom. My dad.

114

Eddie. Childhood girlfriends. And now Fatima. I couldn't wait to take my throne back. He wasn't going to get away with breaking up my family. Fatima was going to come home, whether she liked it or not.

A red Jeep Cherokee pulled onto the shoulder, and rolled along side me. "Excuse me sir, do you need help?"

The woman driving looked well taken care of. She was an all American nip-tuck-it. The first thing I noticed was her large enhancements. Then, I scoped out the huge rock on her ring finger. She was probably an unsatisfied housewife. The look in her eyes told me she was looking for some wild Mandingo which was a good thing, because I could definitely deliver. I searched for kids in the car, but there wasn't any. She was alone. I knew she had some though, because she had a stick figure family plastered on the car window. I wanted to know how bad she wanted Mr. Johnson. So I kept walking, as if I didn't see her.

"Sir. Is everything okay?"

Bingo. I had her. As expected. She rolled with me for awhile. Then, I purposely flashed my missing hand. I figured, I might as well take advantage of my new disability.

"Oh my god.," she clutched her chest, and gasped. The look on her face was priceless. If only she knew, how it happened. She looked horrified. She stopped. Jumped out of the vehicle, and ran to my side. God was good. He sent me good Samaritan at the perfect time.

"Let me see. Are you hurt?" She turned my shoulders and surveyed my body. Who knew the blows Marcus dealt would actually help me. He didn't do a lot of damage. But, the fall out the window had me dented in a few places.

"You poor thing, what happened?" She said, starring at me with crystal blue eyes.

"I got robbed a few miles back. They stole everything. My wallet, keys, and clothes are all gone." I lied. I knew it didn't matter what I said. She wanted to be my white savior, and I was more than happy to let her.

"Come here." She said, leading me to the car. And just like that, I was back in the game.

*****

I was impressed, when we pulled into the driveway. She was laid. All the houses in the addition were at least 14,000 square feet. There had to be money, clothes, a cell phone, and other things I needed inside. Getting equipped was my first step. Finding a way to meet up with Tasha was the next.

At first, I thought it would be tricky getting her to take me home. But it wasn't. I told her some sob story about being a youth minster at a local church. I said a group of young men straight out of juvenile hall took advantage of my kindness, and stole everything, including my car. Painting myself as victim, when I'm bigger than most wide receivers was a stretch, but I couldn't think of a better story at the time. I'm sure my hand gave me a little more credibility. She gave me the side eye when I was trying to fill up wholes in my story, though. She even asked, if I was lying. Instead of answering, I pulled out my dick, and she quickly shut up, and lead me inside.

"Ooh yes, it taste so good," she moaned in between strokes and blows.

Emily was gobbling me up like I was a fountain, and she was dying of thirst. I was getting the best head I had in years. Tasha couldn't even out do her, and that was saying something. My day was obviously going nowhere but up. As far as I was concerned, there was no better time to be a black man in America.

"No hands." I said, throwing her arms to the side.

Her head was banging against the kitchen cabinets, hard. But I didn't let up. I was treating her like the whore she was. The more I slammed against the back of her throat, the louder she moaned. This bitch was definitely a freak. I pulled out. Flipped her over. And fucked her from the behind.

"Who's pussy is this?" I roared.

"Yours. Daddy. Yours." She cried out in pleasure.

"Wrong answer." I pulled her across my lap, and fucked her while standing up. Her long fingernails drug across the length of my back. My skin stung as it was breaking.

"Say my name bitch. Who's pussy is this?" I demanded, pumping away.

"Ooh Marcus! It's your pussy. It's your pussy. Marcus"

Did this bitch just call me Marcus? I let go, and she went crashing onto the floor. I couldn't believe it. He fucked her too. How did he know I was even here? I darted around the kitchen, looking for his ass. He wouldn't get away from me this time. Her stark white kitchen started spinning around me. I couldn't get her voice out of my head. "It's your pussy Marcus," kept playing over, and over again in my head. Did Fatima call out his name when they were fucking too? I bet she did. I pictured myself, punishing her for breaking up our happy family, and running away. This bitch betrayed me too. And I just met her. I wasn't going to forgive her.

"What's the matter baby?" She asked, kissing and rubbing my shoulder.

What do I look like? A fucking fool. She looked up at me, innocently, like I would forget what she said. She could bat her lashes, all she wanted. But I knew the truth. And she did too. I wasn't even going to justify her question with an answer. What's the matter? She knew exactly what she did. I'm tired of having to deal with unfaithful bitches. I bet she thinks I'm going to show her mercy, but I can't. Fatima used it all, already. I gave the bitch an inch, and she took a mile. I'll never make that mistake again. This bitch fucked my brother, and had the audacity to call out his name while I was still in the pussy. Oh yes. She was going to pay.

I swag her around by her elbow. And she laughed. Obviously she thought this was a game. So why shouldn't I play along? I entered her from behind, and pulled her hair. Her oohs and aahs bounced off the kitchen walls. Until, I felt her tighten up to ride the wave. I locked my arm around her neck, just before she climaxed. I held onto my wrist with my good arm, until she no longer struggled. Then, I exploded. Today was definitely going to be a great day.

Chapter 2

Marcus

Police charged through the front door. All of them stood in the middle of my living room with guns and attitudes, ready to fire. Sadly, they just missed the horror that took place, only a few hours ago. Neither of us moved, or said a word. Even though they arrived, we were too exhausted to care. Fatima was curled up on the couch. And I was reclined in my chair.

She looked so broken and disconnected. I was starting to get concerned. We hadn't made eye contact since last night. There was no conversation, or checking of notes. Her pride was too far in the way to let that happen. I tried to wrap my arms around her, but she pushed me away. She made it clear she didn't want to talk, or be comforted. There was nothing I could do to reassure her.

I was so full of angry and rage. I wanted to rip through everything in sight. As her man, it was my job to keep her safe. And I failed. I stayed single after Allison and Jamie died for exactly this reason. I should have protected them. Why wasn't I in the car? If I was driving, things could have ended differently. Maybe they would still been alive, and last night would have never happened.

Either way, I wanted to keep my distance from Fatima to protect her from my bad luck. For whatever reason, those closest to me died. I didn't want that to happen to her. But she was so beautiful and persistent, I couldn't resist her love. It killed me to know, I was the cause of her pain. I brought the boogie man from under her bed. I should have warned her about my past, and sadistic brother. Even though, the media reported him as dead. Deep down, I knew better. The devil could die that easy. All I could do was thank god she was alive, because most people couldn't survive the hell Darius put her through. She had nothing, but my full respect. How she managed to make it while I was incapacitated downstairs, I'll never understand. I couldn't count the times, I came toe to toe with my older brother. I swear next time would be the last though, because one of us was going to die.

If it wasn't for my medical training, last night it would have been me. I fought that bastard with everything I had, but it wasn't enough. He came equipped, and well prepared. I saw nothing but blackness in front of me. But I kept throwing blows. Each time, my fist met steel. Or at least that was what it felt like. I kept alternating my shots. But all of them hit the same thing. It could have been some other defensive material. I didn't know what he was wearing. All I knew was, I couldn't get ahead. My eyes were swelled shut, early in the fight. I was literally swinging from the hip. It didn't take long before I was exhausted, and he had the upper hand. A few left hooks and upper cuts later, he had me on my knees gasping for air. Before I knew it, he was holding my head back, and running a clean blade across my throat. My own brother left me for dead. I knew he was going to find Fatima upstairs, and I couldn't let that happen, but I was fading quick. Then, I remembered there was a first aid kit in one of the bottom kitchen drawers, I just had to find it. I took of my shirt and held it against my neck while feeling my way around the kitchen. Eventually, I found my med pack. I was able to fashion a tourniquet. It stopped the blood from spilling out of my severed jugular vein. It wasn't easy, but I managed to get the job done.

When I was wrapping my neck, I could hear Fatima struggling. I feared she'd be dead, by the time I made it upstairs. Still, I couldn't give up because I could hear her crying. As crazy as it sounds, her uncontrollable sobs and intense wailing gave me strength. I knew if I could hear her voice, she was still alive. On my hands and knees, I drug myself across the living room floor. My body felt so heavy and weak, I questioned my ability to make it to her in time. I felt like passing out, every part of me wanted to lay down and die. But then god showed up. The early morning sun shown through my floor length windows. Call me crazy, but I swear I heard god telling me to get up. So I pulled myself off the ground, and limped up the long staircase.

By the time I reached the second floor I was drained. Even still, I opened the door. To my horror, I saw Satan himself. Darius was tearing into her like some beast from the underworld. Hot streams were pouring down the sides of her eyes, and she wasn't moving or saying anything. It was obvious she was there in body, but not spirit. Rage consumed me. How could I let her down? It was my job to protect her, but I failed to protect her. Just like I did Eddie, Allison, and Jamie. Out of nowhere, an inner strength took over my body. All of sudden I wasn't in pain. I was revved, and ready to go. I charged towards him with everything I had. I sent his ass flying through the two story window like a high powered missile. I prayed for his death, like I'd done several times before. Fatima rushed over and tried to check my wounds, but I wasn't there. The only thing I could see was his demise. Rushing over to the window, I hoped to see his corpse laying in the driveway, but he wasn't there. She peered over my shoulder, and looked down too. I knew she was hoping to see the same thing. When she realized he was gone, she collapsed into a bucket of tears.

We weren't able to call the police immediately. The sadistic bastard planned ahead. I had to get my home phone back online. As soon as I realized Darius was gone. I went outside, flipped the breaker box, and reset the modem in order to call the police. I knew his trail would be ice cold by the time they got here, but I couldn't just give up either. Living two hours out of town had it's benefits, but fast service wasn't one of them. Dammit. I let him get away. Fatima hadn't said a word since he fled from the scene. But I knew what she was thinking. She regretted pushing so hard. She regretted not accepting my rejection when I told her no. She hoped her life could go back to the way it was before she met me. If I could go back in time, I'd protect her from the poison that was me. No one deserved the life I've lived. Especially not a beautiful, and innocent woman like her. I was so lost in my thoughts. I forgot the police had arrived.

"Sir. I'm Officer Moore. We received a call saying there was an intruder in the home?" He spoke matter-of-factually with his hand propped comfortably on his right holster. His gray hair, thick mustache, and staunch posture suggested he was a veteran amongst rookies. I was glad to see they sent a big dog.

"He is already gone. It's been about two hours since he took off. I tried to follow him, but I was too slow." I swept my hands over my injures. It was obvious why I couldn't keep up.

"You say he left over two hours ago. What are we looking for? Did he leave on foot, or by motor vehicle? Any details you can give us will help."

"I can't say. After our tussle downstairs. I limped my way to the second floor and found him. In the middle of …" I couldn't find the words to say what I saw. It was like they were lodged down deep, and I could get a hold of them.

"He was raping me upstairs. Before Marcus came to my rescue. He charged him. And Darius went flying out the window. We both looked out the window, and he was already gone." Fatima answered for me. The room started spinning, and my vision began to fade. I grabbed my neck, and realized my make shift tourniquet was soaked in blood.

"Sir please have a seat.," an EMT said, arriving just in time. I listened from the couch, while Fatima told them what happened.

"Ma'am, you say you knew the assailant," a young officer inquired?

Fatima hesitated. Everything that happened was too much for her. I was used to death and violence. My whole childhood was filled with it, thanks to growing up with a monster. She had no idea how to deal with situations like last night. She must have been in shock, after hearing about what happened to Eddie, last night. When I told her the story, I never dreamed she would ever meet Darius. She couldn't process so much information about someone she never met. Now there asking her more questions about him. I'm sure the facts were more than a little gray.

"Yes officer. That's what she said. She's never met him in person. I told her about him, though." I interjected from the couch.

"Sir, please relax," the blonde working on me said, gently.

"Yes sir. He is correct. Marcus said, he was his brother." Fatima answered.

"Do you remember anything specific about him? Could you see any tattoos, or distinguishable markings on his body?"

"No. But he wore a night vision mask," she answered while looking down at her bloody knuckles.

"When we were fighting downstairs, it felt like he had on armor or something, too." I added.

The officers looked to each other sceptically. Our description of the night's events made him sound like a comic book super villain. But we were telling the truth with no extras.

Office Moore crossed his arms, and said, "Let me get this straight. Neither of you saw his face, but you claim the assailant was a man that was found dead last night?"

I limped across the room and stood inches away

126

from his face. I wasn't going to let him make her or me feel inferior. "Look officer. It has been a long night, and now morning. We've told you everything we know, without any embellishments. If you have any further questions you can reach me at Kids First Pediatrics, I'm the attending physician there, or at home." I knew mentioning I was a doctor would shut the bullshit down fast. I didn't want to deal with anymore crap today.

"No problem, sir. We don't want to give you anymore trouble. We can't treat your brother as suspect for obvious reasons though. I'll have to visit the coroner to make sure the body identified in his home, is in fact his. If it's not, we can consider adding him as a suspect. Rest assured, we'll get to the bottom of this."

I didn't respond. I simply nodded.

Officer Moore tipped his hat, pivoted, and headed out the front door with three rookies following behind him.

"Ma'am. We need to take you in. So we can perform a rape kit." The EMT called out to Fatima.

The look in her eyes told me, she didn't want to go. How could I blame her? I'm sure, it would feel like being raped all over again. "That won't be necessary. I can get everything I need to do the kit from the hospital. I'll send in the results myself." I said directing everyone towards the door. I could

127

see Fatima's shoulders drop in relief.

"Thank you babe," she said, joining me on the couch. It was going to be more than a long couple of days.

Chapter 3

Fatima

With my finger on the trigger, inside of my purse, I opened the door and strolled into my old apartment. Darius wasn't going to catch me off guard again. If he decided to show up, I had six hot ones waiting for his ass in the chamber. I just needed the opportunity to send them flying his way. I replayed all the possible outcomes, before deciding to come here alone. I could have asked Trina, Shana, or Denise to come along, but they would have asked too many questions. Mainly, who was Marcus, and what happened to Darius? I wasn't prepared to answer either question. Of course, Marcus would have been a great support, but I couldn't risk him finding a photo or evidence of me and his brother's relationship. I burned everything I could find, but you never know. I could have forgotten something. It simply wasn't worth the risk.

The last place I wanted to be on earth was here. But I had to make sure the movers got everything out, before I could collect my security deposit. I had only been gone for about a week, but it felt like forever since I'd been inside this house. I looked around, and thought about how happy I used to be living here. Back in the day, things felt so perfect.

Before Darius lost his mind. Before Tasha betrayed me. And before I found out my entire life was lie. The memories were so bitter sweet, I didn't know what to do with them. I just wanted everything from my past to disappear.

The barrage of memories coming my way, made me so grateful to have Marcus in my life. He was kind enough to let me stay with him as long as I wanted. He even offered to have everything packed, moved, and shipped to his place. We only knew each other for about two weeks, but instantly we connected. His generosity amazed me. Before I could ask for what I needed, he already had it in hand. He wanted me to be near him at all times, which was great, because I didn't want to be alone. So it worked. My old self would have felt smothered or overwhelmed. Thank goodness, the naive gullible person I was died with the lies in this house. Even though, our relationship was brand new, my gut told me it was the real thing. I made the mistake of ignoring my intuition in the past, I wasn't going to make the same mistake again.

My footsteps bounced off the empty walls as I walked around my apartment. I saved the worse room for last. I peaked inside the bedroom setup for me and Darius's future baby, and negative emotions consumed me. My stomach twisted into a thousand knots. I felt my breakfast fighting to come up. The thought of having his baby literally made me sick. I

130

told the mover's to sell or throw away all the baby stuff in the house, because I certainly wasn't going to need it. I was relieved to see they did. How could I have been so naive? He didn't even know him. Even though, we lived together for three years. We might as well have been strangers. I certainly learned my lesson. Time wasn't an indication of a healthy relationship. Darius taught me that.

As I turned to leave, I saw something out of the corner of my eye. I pivoted, and nearly fell over. I couldn't believe what I was seeing. Darius was standing on the other side of my patio doors with a wicked grin on his face. My brain didn't know what to do. It was like all my thoughts were caught in a traffic jam, and known of them could switch lanes, or find a way out. I had to be losing my mind. I ran my hand over my face, and shook my head. I hoped I was hallucinating, but I wasn't. He was still standing there laughing at me like this was a game. My palm began to sweat on the grip of the gun, and the steel trigger felt wet in my hand. Was it really him? Or was my eyes playing tricks on me? I couldn't be sure. I kept my eyes closed for a few seconds. Then I opened them again. His was attempting to pull the door open. I wasn't delusional. He was coming to finish the job. Tiny chill bumps ran over my body. He wasn't going to attack me again. I closed my eyes. Aimed. And pulled the trigger.

POP! POP! POP!

CRASH!

Glass went flying everywhere. I opened my eyes, and he was no longer standing there. Where the hell did he go? I dropped the gun in my purse, and ran across the living room. No one was standing on the patio balcony. There was only broken pieces of aluminum and glass on the ground. Across the way, I could see a lonely tree blowing in the wind. Oh my god. It wasn't over. He was stalking me.

BANG! BANG! BANG!

"Open up! It's the police!" A voice yelled from the other side of the door.

"Open up! Or were coming in."

My throat dried up, and I couldn't speak. What the fuck could I say? I knew he was here, but they wouldn't believe me. They didn't even think he was alive. A hawk of a man kicked down the door and bum-rushed inside. Then, he shoved the tip of his gun on my forehead. He peered down at me like he was ready to shot. I was so scared, I couldn't control my bladder.

"Put your hands up. And don't move."

My hands flew up immediately. I wasn't going to question a thing he said. Going to jail wasn't an option. If he asked me to stand on the ceiling, I would have given it a shot, because I wasn't cut out to do time. The officer standing behind him used his gun to motion towards the piss running down my leg. Then the hawk retreated.

"What the hell is going on here?" Officer Moore asked, standing in front of the door.

The trigger happy cop holstered his gun, and began to stammer.

"Spit it out son. What the hell were you doing?" Officer Moore yelled only inches from his face.

I didn't care, what was going on between them. I just wanted to run home and cry. My worst nightmare came true, plus more. Darius was stalking me. And there was nothing I could do about it. Now, I was standing in piss like a psych patient.

"Ms. Butler. I apologize for his reaction, instead of response. These idiots are going to search the premises while we talk. Please explain what happened?"

I crossed my legs at the ankle, and stuttered through my words. "I thought I saw Darius," was all could say.

He looked at me with sympathy in his eyes, then simply shook his head. "Ma'am, have you thought about seeing someone? It's okay to admit you need help. You've been through a lot. It's not easy getting over the type of stuff you've been through."

"I have," I lied. The look he gave me said he wasn't convinced. But thankfully, he didn't push the issue. I didn't want talk to him or anyone else. Darius was standing there smirking at me. I saw him just as clearly as I did Officer Moore, and the other two cops.

"I was planning on giving you and Mr. Du Bois a visit today. We ran the prints at the lab, and the results came back this morning. There is a 99.99 percent chance the man found in the fire was Darius. You don't have to worry about him raising from the ashes ma'am. There is no doubt, he is dead."

"Okay." I wasn't going to tell him he was wrong. The facts weren't up for debate. I'd know his body, scent, and voice anywhere. But I knew it didn't matter what I said. Since he already thought I was crazy. I had to admit, things weren't looking too good for me right now. I didn't give Darius enough credit. He was much smarter than I thought. Somehow, he managed to become the invisible man overnight. Now, there was hardly anything I could do to stay safe.

"Office Miles and Green, are going to follow you home. I'll call maintenance to explain what happened. Please get some rest, and try to recover. It's okay to take some time for yourself. Especially after such a traumatic event."

I nodded, grabbed my purse off the floor, and headed towards the door.

"One more thing ma'am. I'll need your gun."

I gave it to him. Then ran to my car. Embarrassed, didn't explain how I felt.

*****

I pulled into the driveway, and saw Marcus's car. Dammit. Why wasn't he at work? I slammed my hands on the steering wheel in frustration. How was I going to explain the patrol car following behind me, and the smell of piss permeating from my clothes. I got out the car, and prepared to run inside. I would just have to figure out a way to avoid him. Until I got out the shower. Both officers tipped their hats, and leaned against their patrol cars, as I walked inside. They were ordered to setup shop outside of our house, just in case Darius, excuse me, the unknown suspect, decided to comeback. I did feel a little safer knowing they were around.

I crossed my fingers and turned the door knob. Hopefully, he'd be upstairs. As soon as I stepped through the door, he was standing in front of me with a cheesy grin on his face. He was brandishing a piece of paper like it was the winning power ball numbers.

"Welcome home!" he chided.

"Hi." I said, rushing pass him, into the bathroom downstairs. I shut, and locked the door behind me.

"Hey," he followed, and banged on the door. "What's the matter? Have you been peeing like a Russian race horse?" He still had an annoying laugh in his voice. What hell was there to be happy about. I wasn't in the mood for jokes.

I pulled off my clothes, and I turned on the water. I wasn't in the mood to talk. Once I was out of the shower. I wrapped in a thick white towel, and realized I didn't have any clean clothes to put on. When I came out, he was sitting in his favorite chair. He definitely wasn't looking enthusiastic anymore.

"I'm sorry about what happened earlier. The officers explained why you were in such a shitty mood, when you came home." He clasped my hands, and lead me to the couch.

"You don't have anything to be sorry about. You didn't know what happened. And I was too embarrassed to tell you." I hated making him feel bad. Marcus was such a good man. If only he knew, I didn't deserve his kindness. I didn't tell him about me and Darius, the plan to con him, or anything else. He was still convinced the other night was his

136

fault, because of the bad blood between them. But I knew the truth. Darius was coming to make good on his promise. In his world, I was his property, and Marcus stole me away. He swore he'd never let me go. And I believed him.

Marcus smiled weakly, but didn't respond. It was obvious, I sucked the happiness right out of him. He seemed excited to talk when I came home. Maybe telling me the good news would lift his mood. I can't image anything positive coming out of this situation, though.

"Fatima, you trust me don't you?" he said, breaking my thoughts.

"Of course."

"Good." His gripped my hands tightly and looked down at them. His serious attitude was really starting to freak me out. What the hell did he want to say.

"Marcus. Just tell me already. It's been a long day. You're going to give me a heart attack."

"I got the kit results today." Oh my god. He gave me the monster. I knew it. Darius was fucking around with that nasty bitch Tasha. There was no telling what that bitch had.

"I have HIV. I can't believe it." tears started rolling down my face.

"No … No. babe. Are you crazy. You're clean.

We're going to have a baby." I swear the words left his lips in slow motion. I was happy to find out I didn't have any diseases, but relief and joy didn't overtake my body. Instead I felt fear and regret. I was with both of them so close together. It would be impossible to determine which one was the father.

"Aren't you excited."

I threw my hands around his neck, and hugged him tightly. I couldn't bare lying to him anymore. We both held each other, and cried for different reasons. What the hell was I going to do with a baby?

Chapter 4

Fatima

No one came out of the building the same. I watched from across the street as women dodged past protestors carrying signs, and bibles in their hands. Some entered as aggressively as the people demonstrating outside. Others held their head down in shame. I knew which category I'd fall under. Abortion was never an option to me, but I was definitely pro-choice. I certainly didn't agree with the government making medical decisions. I just never considered it an option for myself, especially considering my family background.

I should have been grateful to be pregnant. I setup a room for my imaginary baby, and even spent hundreds of dollars preparing for him or her. So why couldn't I imagine carrying to full term? I couldn't even picture myself being a mom, anymore. Plus, I wanted to be married before getting pregnant. Now, I was no different than those chicks on Maury. I didn't know if Marcus or Darius was the father of my child. I couldn't even say the reality out loud, I was so ashamed. What would I do, if Darius was the father?

Most of the time, I spent with him was amazing.

I couldn't lie. It was the truth. As much as it pained me to admit it. Looking back, I still didn't understand what happened to him. At some point, he turned into a different person. On second thought, he wasn't even human anymore to me. He was just a beast, or personal tormentor that wouldn't set me free. The possibility of this being his child was too much to bare. How could I carry such a thing inside of me? Rationally I knew it wasn't the baby's fault, but my heart wouldn't believe it. I still screamed his name, in my sleep. The things he did to me I could never forget. How could I move on, if I had to look at his child's face everyday? I didn't know if I could.

There was no way, I could have created a better hell for myself. How the hell did I fuck up my life so bad? Marcus was an innocent victim. He didn't even know half of what was going on. Every time he woke up in the middle of the night to buy me chocolate mint ice cream, because I was having a pregnancy craving, I wanted to scream, "The baby isn't yours. I'm a piece of shit. You should leave me." If I had a moral bone in my body, I would say just that, and paid the consequences. The problem was I needed him. I couldn't survive without him. The night terrors, and panic attacks were getting so bad. I rarely left the house. I was either scared Marcus would find out about our relationship, or Darius would pop up and kill me. Getting an abortion would probably be the best thing for everyone involved, including the baby. This child couldn't survive the mess I created. There was no other choice, I had to go through with it. Marcus shouldn't be tied down to me, because of what I did. He deserved someone honest and decent, not a liar like me.

I walked into the clinic, and saw women of every shade. Some even had swollen bellies. I was surprised to see them there, because I felt bad already being three months along. You couldn't tell I was pregnant, though, because of my height. I signed in, and sat down with the rest of the woman, who were scared to death.

"Fatima," the receptionist called from behind the counter. I said a silent prayer, and followed her to the examination room.

*****

"Welcome home!" everyone shouted when I walked through the door. Confetti and horns blew in my face. I was so caught off guard, I nearly jumped out of my skin. Marcus had completely out done himself. The living room was filled with yellow and gray balloons. It looked like a cute bubble bee convention. There was bubble cake, juice, cups, and plates. I couldn't have decorated better myself. I scanned the room, and saw my old friends standing in the back. How did Marcus find them? Trina, Shana, and Denise rushed over to give me hug. I could tell they were genuinely happy to see me.

"Do you like it?" he asked, pulling me into a warm embrace.

"I do. Thank you. You didn't have to do this."

"Of course, I did. I want you to be happy."

Looking around the room, I realized half the people I didn't even know. Still, the thought was sweet. I recognized Amy from his office, and of course the girls, but everyone else were complete strangers.

"Tell me the truth. Is this okay?" he asked, motioning around the room. "It seems like you've been having a hard time. I hope you're not mad, I invited everyone over. I thought you should have some fun without worrying. So, I brought the party to you. Besides, I wanted to tell everyone about the baby. I couldn't keep the secret anymore."

"Of course, I'm not mad. I do have to use the bathroom though." I pecked him on the cheek, handed him my bag, and escaped to the upstairs bathroom. I could feel a panic attack coming on.

God, I hated getting setup. If I wanted Denise, Trina, and Shana to know my business I would have told them. The last thing I wanted to come home to was a roomful of people. I could careless if I knew them or not, I just wanted to be left alone. Marcus was always surprising me with something sweet. He meant well, but this time he was completely off the mark. I didn't want to celebrate anything. Especially not pregnancy. I wanted to come home, and zone out on trash television. Now I had to deal with this shit. Yeah, he was trying to do something sweet for me, but it only made me feel worse. I needed some space to figure my shit out.

Boom! Boom! Boom!

"What?" I yelled. Someone was beating on the door like they lost their damn mind.

"Open up Fatima!"

I swung the door open, and saw Marcus was pissed. His eyes were razor sharp, and he looked like he was on a war path.

"What the hell is this?" I was literally speechless. He was thrusting my appointment card from the clinic in my face. It must have fallen out of my bag, when I handed it to him. I was in such a hurry to get upstairs, I must have dropped it. I could hear people saying their goodbyes, and leaving downstairs. Apparently, he was ready to fight.

"Answer me. What is this, Fatima?"

"Baby, let me explain." My mind was racing, I

143

had no idea what to say. I just knew I needed to say something. So he would calm down.

"Go ahead. I'm listening."

I was still drawing a blank. Anything I said, wouldn't sound good. He was pissed, and had every right to be. "It's not what it looks like babe." I couldn't think of anything better. He threw his hand up, and cut me off.

"You want to kill our child Fatima. Why? What the hell did I ever do to you?" he stood in the doorway with tears in his eyes. I really fucked up this time. The last thing I wanted to do was hurt him. I scheduled the appointment, because I didn't want to get in his way. How could explain my situation. I could tell him Darius forced me to date him, that the only reason we met was so I could con him out of his inheritance, or that I couldn't refuse because he threatened to rape me, if I didn't fall in line. None of those answers would make him feel better. So why tell him? Instead, I lied. It was kinder.

"Marcus, I'm sorry. I don't know what else to say. I was stupid. I made a mistake."

He got on his knees, and placed his ear against my belly. "Please tell me you didn't do it, Fatima. I need both of you to keep me going. I can't handle anymore bullshit." I'd never seen Marcus cry. Even after the attack, he didn't shed a tear. I really felt like a piece of shit for what I did.

"I didn't do it. Marcus. The baby is okay."

"Thank god." he said, wrapping his arms around my waist. He was breathing so hard, I could feel his heart beating against my thigh.

"I'm sorry, baby. I know you've been through a lot too. I didn't want to add to your stress. I thought, your life would be easier, without us."

He stood up, and grabbed my face with both of his hands. "Listen to me Fatima. I don't want you to go anywhere. You're my family. It's just me, you, and this baby." he said, putting his hand on my stomach. "I need you to believe that. Yeah. We had a rocky start. But our love is real. If we can survive that night, our relationship is ironclad, and unbreakable." He squeezed me like he was I afraid I would disappear.

I wanted to deserve everything he said, but the truth was I didn't. Even my body rejected his words. My chest was so tight, and full of tears, I just refused to let any of them fall. He treated me like fine china, not realizing I was the one responsible for his pain. His generosity and love, only made me feel worse. Darius couldn't hurt Marcus directly. He would have seen him coming. He needed me to play my part in order to solve his legal problems. If I stole the money, and returned to Darius like he wanted. Marcus wouldn't have gotten hurt. We would be living in separate houses. And this baby wouldn't exist. Instead, I've entangled him in Darius's web. There was no way he would leave us alone, now that I'm pregnant. Finding out would only fuel his fire. I couldn't bare lying to him anymore. I needed to tell him the truth. He didn't love me. He only thought he did. He didn't know why we met, or what my intentions were that night.

"Marcus, I have something to tell you. I hope you can understand why I went to the clinic."

"You don't have to explain anything to me Fatima. I just want you promise you'll take care of our child."

My voice started to shake, but I wasn't going to stop now. He needed to hear what I had to say. "That's the thing. I went to the clinic, because I didn't know if you or Darius was the father of my baby."

"Fatima. Stop worrying. There's no way Darius is the father. The blood work showed your were already a few weeks pregnant, the night of the attack. We're good. Just be happy, okay." He planted a soft kiss on my lips, and hugged me tight. I couldn't believe his response. My willpower was gone. I couldn't muster up the strength to say it again. So, I left it at that.

Chapter 5

Marcus

AAH!

Jarred out of my sleep, I shot up in bed. Damn. I hadn't gotten a good night's sleep in months, which was really starting to wear on me. I had to hire a partner to take over some of my patients at work. Even though, I hated to do it. I had no other choice. I kept having to run home because she needed me. The panic attacks were nonstop. They consumed her day and night. Nothing seemed to help. As much as I want to understand where she was coming from, it was difficult. The attack happened over six months ago. I knew how bad it was. I was there, but I thought we could commemorate, but she wouldn't even talk to me about it. I even offered to pay for therapy, medication, or whatever she needed, but she refused to go. I didn't know what the hell to do. I even bought a shot gun, rifle, and .45 to make her feel safer. But none of it seemed to restore her faith in me.

"No! No!" Her bone chilling scream filled the room. I was shaking her arm, but she wasn't waking up.

"Fatima! Fatima! I'm here. Do you here, babe?

Wake up." I rubbed her forehead, when she was coming to. She was so into the dream, her body was drenched in sweat. I rubbed her swollen belly, and felt our little girl squirm. I hoped to god, she wasn't as stressed out as her mom.

"Marcus." Fatima sighed deeply. I could feel the stress lifting off her shoulders, and onto mine. Within seconds, she feel back to sleep. It was like a revolving door. The same thing happened last night, and the night before that, and so on. This shit had to stop.

I moseyed down the staircase, then poured myself a shot of whiskey. What else could I do? I wasn't much of a drinker, or at least I didn't used to be. But lately, I'd been reaching for the bottle more, and more. I guess the stress was getting to me. Even though, Darius had apparently disappeared, his presence was still felt. Fatima was consumed with him. I couldn't even take my own woman out. Every time I suggested going out for dinner, a movie, or even a stroll down the street, she would flip out and start talking about bumping into him. I got a license to carry. I knew the area. I was capable of protecting her, and our baby. Why couldn't she have faith in me? I took another swig of whiskey, and thought about the state of my life. I would never lose my woman and child again. I wish she could understand that.

Life gave me another chance to prove I could

148

keep my family safe. And I was determined to succeed this time. I knew I made mistakes in the past, but I wouldn't repeat them. The night Darius took Eddie out, I was awake. I could have gotten out of bed, and told him to stop – but I was too much of a coward, even back then. It shouldn't have mattered he was crazy. I should have met him every step of the way. Instead, we hardly talked, even though we shared room. I got so freaked out, because of the crazy shit he did like stuffing our cat inside the dryer. Then, turning it on. I still remember the smell of our cat's rotting flesh. It never got out of the walls, no matter how much my mom tried to clean it. Regardless, I could have at least tried to stop him. Even if he beat my ass like he usually did. Worst case scenario, my parents would have woken up, and Eddie would still be alive. Darius was only a year older than me, but he was six years older than Eddie. I should have been his protector. He didn't stand a chance scraping with him. He was just a little kid. I slammed my fist on the table, and I doubled up. It was the only thing that could take the edge off the pain.

"Baby, is everything okay?" she asked, standing across the room. She looked even more beautiful carrying my child than she did before. My heart swelled up just thinking about her.

"I'm fine," I said, trying to steady my words. I definitely didn't want to give her anything else to worry about.

"What's wrong baby?" she wrapped her arm around my neck, and rubbed my chest. I could never lie to her. She always knew when something was wrong.

"Don't worry about me. Worry about you." I planted a soft kiss on her lips. "And our little princess." I said, kissing her belly button.

"Marcus, come to bed." She tried to pull me off the bar stool, but I wasn't going anywhere. I couldn't waking up to her screams. It was driving me crazy.

"I'll be right behind you babe. Go ahead without me."

"You said that last night. And I found you asleep on the couch in the morning."

"Fatima please. Just go back to bed." She crossed her arms. I knew then, getting her to go back to sleep wasn't going to be easy.

"I don't know what's gotten into you lately. You've hardly been eating. You don't want to come to bed anymore. Tell me what's wrong."

She asked for the truth, but I knew she couldn't handle it. I couldn't remember the last time we made love. Every time, I touched her, she pulled away. It was like I repulsed her. When I brought it up to her in the past, she blamed it on the pregnancy, but I saw the look on her face. Her eyes were wide and full of terror. It was like she was looking into the eyes of a monster. I couldn't help wondering if she saw him when she looked in my eyes. We do look similar, as much as I hated to admit. It felt like she wasn't even mine. Like I was sleeping with another man's woman, with his woman, not mine. Even though, I was the one running her bath water, rubbing her swollen feet, and feeding her when she was hungry. He still had her heart clutched in his fist, and I couldn't get to it. No matter how hard I tried.

"Babe. I don't want to do this tonight. Just go back to bed."

"Do what Marcus? What is this? I just want to know what's wrong?"

"What isn't wrong Fatima? You can't sleep without waking up screaming. You haven't left the house since what happened. We don't have sex. I don't even remember what it feels like. But you want to know what's wrong." I slammed down my shot glass, and paced the floor. I didn't want to do this with her.

"So all this is because of me? Why didn't you just say so, huh? I don't have to stay here, if you don't want me to. I can leave." Her eyes welled up with tears, and her fingers started trembling. We both knew, she had no place to go.

151

"I'm not saying everything is your fault … a man has needs. It's as simple as that." Before she came into my life, I was celibate. But that was different. I wasn't thinking about love, sex, or relationship. I was completely engulfed in my work. Laying with her at night was torture. I wanted to kiss her sweet lips, full breasts, and that honey pot between her legs, but every time I tried, it turned into a fight.

"So your punishing me, because I won't have sex with you?" I couldn't believe it. Was she smoking crack. Everything I did was for her. I came downstairs, because I didn't want to disturb her, and that made me selfish.

"Are you out of your mind? What do you want me to do Fatima?"

"Come to bed."

"I can't take it anymore. You're driving me crazy." Instantly, her face was filled with sadness. I didn't want to fight. I just needed a break. Fatima stood there with tears in her eyes. I had to make things better for the both of us.

"Come here." I said, pulling her into my chest. I brushed her hair as she cried in my arms. We were both such a fucking mess. The last year was bitch. I wanted to be strong for the both of us, but it was hard. It seemed like everyday was battle. It didn't help that she reminded me so much of my mom which really scared the hell out of me. I didn't want her to meet the same fate.

After Darius killed my Eddie. Our family was destroyed. He was shipped off to juvenile hall, but he wasn't the only one punished. It was like we all died right along with Eddie. My dad was never home. He lived at the church, but he wasn't only there to deliver the good news. No. Half the congregation had a piece of Mr. Du Bois and everybody knew it. We constantly had woman volunteering to clean our house, wash our clothes, and cook dinner. They said it was to help the first lady, but I knew what was up. I couldn't count the times I found my dad in compromising positions. My poor mom was too gone to even notice. As a kid, I hated my dad. I couldn't understand how cheated. As a man, I could honestly say, I didn't blame him. He still had needs. Besides, being around my mom was unbearable. She just wasn't the same after his death. In fact, she wasn't even a shell of her former self. All she did was reminisce or hallucinate about the good old days. My dad tried his best to stand by her, but nothing he tried helped. She was prescribed all kinds of medications. All of them, she abused. Half the time, I expected to find her dead when I came home from school. But somehow, she survived. I didn't understand how she outlived my old man. I refused to let history repeat itself. Fatima would have to get better. She had no other choice. Our baby deserved the best, and neither of us were up to par at the

153

moment.

Fatima whipped her face, and looked into my eyes. "I promise to do better, okay," she actually looked sincere. I'm sure she'd try, but I certainly wasn't going to get my hopes up. After all, we were technically still in the honeymoon faze, and we had already been through so much. If this was the good times, I definitely didn't want to see the bad. I'd support her as much as I could. Hopefully, she'd make good on her word.

Chapter 6

Darius

Tasha spread out the foil, dropped the crystal, lit it, and inhaled like a champion. I smacked her bare ass lying across the bed, and she turned around holding a ball of smoke in her mouth. She pressed her lips against mine, and exhaled. We'd been charging, and fucking all night. I felt like a kid again. I surveyed her body, and had to admit, she looked amazing after having three kids. Her body was stacked and fat ass fuck. A nigga couldn't hold a nut, messing around with her. She was a certified freak. The girl practically lived on her knees. Don't get it twisted, I for damn sure wasn't complaining. But, her ass was what drove me wild. I shook my head just thinking about that donkey sitting on her back. I'd been chilling with her for the last few weeks to recuperate from the madness. I needed to come up with another game plan. A little ass, and a hint of smoke was just what I needed to get my mind right. I grabbed another handful, before sitting up to watching the nightly news.

Officers found Emily Bronson face down and nude inside her Rose Creek Addition home. Neighbors, family, and friends haven't been able to provide deputies with any plausible suspects.

*Crimes like this never happen in this neighborhood.
No one knows what to think. A candlelight vigil will
be held later tonight in her memory. People in the
community describe her as a great mother, wife,
friend, and community pillar. She was an active
PTA member, and volunteer at New Beginning
Ministries. No one can understand how an
outstanding citizen like her was attacked so
brutally. Let alone in her own home. Police weren't
able to find any signs of forced entry. It appears,
she knew her attacker well enough to invite him or
her inside. Sadly, her husband and three children
found her manned body, after returning home.
Here is a few words from her grieving spouse.*

*Emily didn't deserve this. I can't believe
someone would do such a thing to her. She was
innocent. And a good person. Why did she have to
die so young. (Inaudible) If you have any
information that can help police find her killer,
please, pickup the phone now. Don't wait. We need
your assist immediately, while the trail is still hot.
We can't afford to let this monster run free on the
streets.*

I clicked off the television and laughed.
Television was definitely the right word. They were
certainly telling visions, because that broadcast was
full of lies. I'm sure Emily was a lot of things, but
innocent, for damn sure wasn't one of them. I
usually have to blaze a trail for Mr. King Snake, but

156

her road was already paved, and ready to go. The bitch did give phenomenal head though.

"Momma when is Tavia and Nikki coming back?" little man asked with his cup in hand. I could always depend on four things from Tasha: good food, nice smoke, mediocre pussy, and lip. Being an acceptable mother to my son, wasn't on the list. I couldn't trust her to raise him right. She had her nappy-headed kids beating him up everyday. They had to go. Those little bitches weren't going to be shit anyway. They were just taking up space. Besides, I wasn't trying to be around another niggas kids, anyway. What type of girls hit on their little brother? They were acting like dikes, and hadn't even left the nest yet. I gave Tasha two options: she could drop them off somewhere, or allow me to handle the situation. As expected, she had them, and their shit packed in flash.

"Momma," he continued to whine. She didn't respond. Her sandy brown her was laid out and covering her face. She didn't have any clothes on. Neither of us did. She was butt naked, and faced down on the bed. Everywhere you looked, shit was thrown. Tasha's room was always a pit. I pushed on the back of her head, but she didn't move. Was this stupid bitch dead?

"Tasha! Tasha!" I yelled, but she didn't respond. DeMarcus started screaming and crying. The plate on the night stand didn't have any dope on it. A pool of frothy drool was in her mouth.

"Get out!" I yelled, while flipping her over. He ran behind me, and starting screaming even louder. I flung his ass against the wall. He didn't need to see what was going on. Besides, I didn't have time to explain shit him, at the moment. Tasha was burning up. I couldn't let her die. I still need her help to fulfill my plan.

I ran to the bathroom, and filled up the tub with cold water. I needed to shock her system. We had a couple of bags of ice in the freezer, I decided to throw them inside too. A ran back to the room, threw her over my shoulder, and dumped her in the tub.

She started flopping like a fish immediately. I sighed in relief. I thought she was dying. I couldn't have her stupid ass, ruining my plans. She was holding onto the side of the tub, trying to catch her breath. I put her in a headlock, until her face turned purple.

"If you ever do that shit again, I'll kill you, okay?" A tear rolled down her eye, and she nodded with the quickness. I let her ass go, and she quickly grabbed at her neck. Her bright complexion returned to her face. And little man ran into the room, and threw his arms around her. I hated for him to see his mom like that. But I couldn't let her ruin my plans.

Everything in my life was perfect, before I started messing with her ass. Business was great. Me and Fatima were looking forward to our life together. Everything was really looking up. Every now and again, I had to deal with the voices in my head, but that wasn't anything new. They'd been with me since I was a little kid. I learned how to keep them in check. They rarely caused problems or affected my daily life.

If it wasn't for Fatima's bright idea, life would still be good right now. She just couldn't wait to introduce me to Tasha. I remember the day we met. As soon as I saw her, I knew they weren't related. Fatima was tall, slender, and top heavy. She looked like a model. Tasha on the other hand, looked like a your typical video ho. They both looked good, but served different purposes. Fatima was the type you brought to Christmas parties, and conferences. Tasha was definitely a side chick, or back burner at best. I knew Tasha was trouble as soon as I saw her. It wasn't the body that gave it away. It was her demeanor. She had slut written all over her. Fatima was just too naive to see it. She didn't have any respect for her. Her breast were always spilling out of her tops. I don't think I every saw her wearing anything, but skinny jeans that displayed every dangerous curve she possessed. Bringing her around was like putting a smoked Christmas ham in front of starved dog. Anybody would have taken a bite.

I remember the first day Fatima introduced us. Her face lit up when she talked about her girl. She even called Tasha her sister. Apparently, they roomed together as teenagers, since they were both runaways. Fatima was tired of living in shelters and boarding houses. As soon as she hit puberty, no one wanted to take her on as a foster child. She was tall, and developed early. Women didn't want her in their home. It would have been too much temptation for their sons and husbands. I couldn't blame them. My girl was sexy as fuck. That was why she decided to pack her shit, and hit the streets. Somewhere along the way she met Tasha.

From what she told me, Tasha's background was no better. Her mom had men running in and out the house. Many of them paid Tasha a visit when the lights went out. She tried to tell her mom, but she didn't care. She just kept on doing her thang. You'd think Tasha would decide to be better than her mom. Nope. Instead, she became just like her. Word got around, she'd do anything for a price. Shortly after, she became pregnant. After the second time, her mom put her out on the streets. Soon after, she met Fatima. They were inseparable until I came along.

As bad as the story sounds, the fault didn't lie with me. Tasha was the master pulling the strings. I was a victim like Fatima. Anytime she left us alone, Tasha was on my nuts. At first it was subtle. She'd accidentally spill her drink in my lap. Then, she'd seductively clean me off. When Fatima got back, she would jumped up, of course. Somehow, she never got caught. Every time she approached me, I turned her down, but she only got more aggressive. She started calling me randomly for help. For example, her car broke down. So, she hit me up. She claimed I was the only one who could help her, because she didn't have a man in her life. Yeah right. I knew game when I saw it, but I went anyway. Her tire had a clean slash it. It couldn't have happened naturally. But I didn't crack her face. Actually, I thought it was funny. So I kicked her some cash, and put on her spare tire. Fatima never heard a word about it. I felt a little bad for not telling her, but it wouldn't have done anything but raise suspension. Alright. I admit, we fucked occasionally. But it was nothing serious. So I kept our little meetings to myself. I knew, I was wrong, but she needed my help. I couldn't leave a single mother stranded on the side of the road. At first, I was able to keep her in line without a problem. But then, my operation blew up.

When Eddie got arrested. I couldn't take the stress. I tried turning to Fatima for support, but she didn't get it. She kept going on about having a baby, and getting married. I couldn't think about family planning when I had my freedom on the line. There were many things I loved about her. She was different than most woman I met. She didn't let bad experiences sour her sweetness. Even though, she didn't have family, she was the most nurturing person I ever met, next to my mom. I knew she'd be a perfect mother and wife someday. It just wasn't the right time. If only she understood that. Unfortunately, her head was too much in the clouds. She couldn't be there for me at the time. I had to look elsewhere for support.

My boy Tool was good at following directions. But his slow ass couldn't think his way out of a paper bag. So he wasn't any help. Then there was Tasha. She understood how gritty life could be. Sometimes life forced your hand to do things others wouldn't understand. When I was on the edge, she came to me barring everything I needed to decompress. The first time we got together, she rolled up a fatty laced with angle dust, and we conceived little man. I was enraged. I swore I'd never touch that shit again. But life got too hectic, and I reached for it again. For awhile, crystal was my girl. She calmed me down, and I was able to think clearer than before. But then, everything got worse. The voices in my head weren't listening. In fact, they got louder, and louder, until I couldn't control them anymore. If I would have stayed away from this bitch, things wouldn't have snowballed. I would be on top of the world, like I was before I met her ass. As far as I'm concerned, she orchestrated this whole situation. Now, it was her responsibility to fix it.

Chapter 7

Darius

"The receptionist said, she's six months along. They threw a baby shower and everything." Tasha said, sucking her teeth and crossing her arms.

I was overjoyed. Fatima was going to have my baby. I reached across the stick shift, and hugged her tightly. We were finally back on track. "Did you get a chance to see her? Is she big? I bet she doesn't even look pregnant? My girl always looks sexy as fuck?"

"She looked alright." She rolled her eyes, then stared out the window.

I backed handed her ass. "Bitch, I don't you need you putting dubs on shit. Just answer my fucking questions." I wanted to track Fatima myself, but after the incident at her apartment. I decided to back off. I didn't want her getting arrested, or shooting my ass. I had to be practical.

"I'm sorry." She yelled, grabbing her face.

Every once and awhile, Tasha got lippy. I had to make sure to keep her in line. Looking at her now, you couldn't tell she used to be fine. Her body was no longer thick. The dope was taking a toll on her

164

beauty. I was seriously thinking about restricting her use. She needed to thicken up.

"Don't hit my mommy!" DeMarcus yelled, from the back seat.

"Punk, shut up." I said, laughing. I pushed him back in his seat, and started smoking a laced blunt. He little ass thought he was hard.

Tasha had been doing recon missions for awhile. DeMarcus had to go to his well child appointment. It was the perfect opportunity to get information on Fatima. I knew Fatima didn't tell Marcus about our plan to con him out of his money. If she did, I'm sure they wouldn't be together. Fatima had to be scared, because Tasha never saw her visiting Marcus at work. Apparently, she knew me better than I thought. I'd never give up on us. We were family. The fact that Marcus thought he could steal my girl, only made the game sweeter.

I needed to find away to move closer to her, without alerting the police. I wasn't about to let him raise my child. I wondered, if we were having a boy or girl. She always said, she wanted a little Darius. The memory brought a smile to my face. The mission was taking longer than I expected, but news of her pregnancy got my creative juices flowing again. I decide to make myself known.

"Did you find out anything else?" I asked, taking a long drag. Tasha wasn't paying attention. She was too busy picking at the soars on her arms. Her beauty was gone. Now the drugs were working on her mind. She wouldn't be any use for much longer. "Tasha. Did you find out anything else?" I repeated, agitated?

"I told you everything already. The receptionist didn't know anything else. I couldn't' even schedule a follow up appointment with Marcus. DeMarcus will have to see a new doctor the next time, he comes in. So I didn't schedule another appointment.

"Good girl," I said, passing the blunt. I found out everything I needed to make my next move. With Fatima being so far along, he'd be staying at home. So I couldn't strike there. It wasn't worth trouble striking at home. I'd have to get her another way. I'd been waiting to catch her outside, but she wasn't leaving the nest. I just had to stay patient. Eventually, she'd slip up. When she did, I'd be waiting in the cut.

Marcus left for work about thirty minutes ago. I was posted on the main road from their house. Today was going to be the day I saw my girl again. I had Tasha befriend some of Fatima's old girlfriends from college on Facebook. She thought I didn't know about the nights she went partying with the girls, but I knew. I just wasn't showing her my full hand. I figured it was a calculated risk worth taking. She could have caught wind and closed down all her social media accounts, and I would have been without some valuable information. Thankfully I got lucky, and was provided with a healthy stream information. Not because of what she posted though. She hadn't been online for months. Her girlfriend Shana, on the other hand, basically posted whenever she took a shit. I knew their full schedule for the day, just from reading her public wall. They had food and shopping on the agenda today. So I planned on tagging along. It had been too long, since I paid my baby a visit.

Fatima pulled onto the main road, and I followed four car lengths behind her. I didn't want to rush back into her life just yet. Instead, I decided to gently make my presence known. She needed to remember some of the good times we had together, not just the bad. I could have easily kidnapped or forced her to be with me, but I didn't want to do that.

I wanted to show her how tough life would be with Marcus, or anyone else. She needed to learn from her mistakes, by dealing with the consequences of her actions. She needed to understand, why deciding to leave was a bad choice. And I planned on showing her why. I asked myself regularly, what the fuck was wrong with her? Why couldn't she understand how easy life would be, if we were together? She wouldn't have to live with her head on a swivel. She could relax and enjoy her life, knowing she was safe with me. I really loved her stupid ass, but she could be too stubborn at times. Unfortunately, she would have to learn her lessons the hard way. Lucky for her, I took an individualized approach. For months, I spent my time developing the perfect curriculum. I knew exactly what she needed to see the light. Strong motivation, direction, and a desirable reward would have her ass begging to come back home.

Fatima pulled into a plaza parking lot. There was a Korean nail shop, a liquor store, and other miscellaneous shops inside. She was there meeting her girlfriends at a home style diner. I'd eaten there a few times, an old white couple owned the place. They had the best yeast rolls, cornbread, and chicken around. My stomach started growling just

168

thinking about the menu. She walked through door, and I thumbed through the Sunday paper while I waited. The diner was too small for me surveillance from inside. She would have immediately seen me coming if I went inside. The cover story read:

The Good Wife Killer

Authorities have connected three homicides with the murder that took place six months ago in Rose Creek Addition. Three other victims were found with the same signature. All three victims were happily married with children, and members of affluent neighborhoods. The first victim Emily Bronson was just thirty six years old, and found dead in her kitchen. The second victim Crystal Montgomery was a twenty eight year old, mother of two. She was found dead in her master bedroom. The last victim Barbara West was thirty two years old. She had three kids, and was found dead in the guest bedroom. We can't release details about the killer's signature. Police have received several false leads due to incorrect information, and copy cat attempts ...

The article continued, but I read enough. They weren't even close to being on the right track. I needed to send a thank you card to whoever decided to follow my lead, cause I didn't know any of the other bitches. Killing Emily was a simple solution to a complex problem. I wasn't anybody's serial killer, though. In fact, I was insulted at the implication. If I wanted to start slaying people, I wouldn't just go after boring bitches in the burbs. Where's the fun in that? Why make it obvious by going after the same type of bitches? The Good Wife Killer. That shit sounded corny ass fuck. They could have come up with something better than that. Regardless. It felt good knowing, I was still the invisible man.

I was surprised the media was making such a big deal out of Emily's death. I couldn't turn on the television, computer, or radio without somebody talking about finding her killer. They acted like the bitch was finding the cure to cancer. I rubbed my hands over the front of the paper. There was a large photo of Emily and her family on the front. I folded the rest of the people out of the frame, and reminisced about the time we spent together. The way her body jerked before taking her last breath was better than any drug, or bitch on the street. A warm sensation covered my body, as I allowed myself to relive the experience. The idea of another kill did sound good to me. In fact, just thinking about it made my dick hard. I had a thirst for more of the same, but that shit would have to wait for now, because I couldn't lose sight of my goal.

While Fatima was busy grubbing, and chopping it up with her friends, I decided to leave her a little present, for when she came back. I hopped out the car, and crept up to her vehicle. I picked up a

greeting card, and wrote a special note inside. I
wanted to let her know, I was excited about our
new bundle of joy.

HONK! HONK! HONK!

The car went fucking bonkers. I fell on my ass,
dropped the card, and jerked my head from side to
side. I barely touched the fucking thing, and it
started flipping out. All I did was try to slide the
card in the lip of the window. I put it back in my
pocket, and jetted across the parking lot, before
anyone could come rushing out. I peered through
the blacked out windshield from the drivers seat. I
watched Fatima, she was only a few steps behind
me, and her friends quickly followed behind her.
She cupped her mouth, and threw her hands on top
of her head. I didn't want to upset her. It wasn't
good for the baby. I just wanted to let her know, I
was excited to meet him or her. Besides her being
upset, she looked more beautiful than I
remembered. She had one of those sweater style
maternity dresses on, and she wore her hair pulled
up in a high bun. I watched as she surveyed the
parking lot. I'm sure she was looking for me.

What the hell was going on? My eyes were bulging
out of my head in shock. If my eyes weren't
deceiving me, it appeared light was reflecting off
her finger. I saw it again! I couldn't believe it. This
muthafucker bought her a ring. I slammed my
hands against the stirring wheel, and started

punching the dashboard. Not only did he steal her from me, but he's trying to claim my child, and marry her ass, too. Oh hell nawl, this shit wasn't happening. He had me all the way fucked up. Shit just got real. I definitely needed to switch up my game plan. Since fourth quarters was over. And we were now in overtime. This game was too tight to call. I fucked around for way too long. It was time to wrap this shit up, asap.

Chapter 8

Fatima

"What the hell do you want?" I was pissed. I couldn't believe she had the nerve to show her face. Tasha was standing on my front porch, looking as pitiful as ever. She even had DeMarcus with her. I guess she figured, pulling on my heart strings would further her cause. I have to admit, it did a little bit, because if she was by herself, I would have slammed the door in her face already.

"I know, I'm the last person you want to see right now, but I have something important to tell you." Whatever she had to say, couldn't be important, because I could careless about what was going on in her life. I didn't know if the pregnancy hormones were getting to me, but I wasn't as mad as I put on. I never saw her look so bad in my life. I had my own problems to deal with. I didn't need her adding to my list of shit to do. Actually, that wasn't entirely true. She used to be so vivacious and lively. She never left the house without doing her hair and makeup. She actually ragged on me for not wearing the latest fashions like she did. Honestly, I looked better than her, even though I was six months pregnant. Something really had to be wrong for her to show up on my door step. Especially considering she looked so bad.

I stepped to the side, motioning for her to come in. I knew, I probably shouldn't have, but I still cared about her. Even though, she betrayed me. We used to be so close. I thought we'd grow old together, and reminisce about the good old days while talking in our rocking chairs. Her betrayal totally blind sided me. I really thought we were more than friends. It was crazy how our entire relationship collapsed over a piece of shit like Darius. I would've been a blessing if she met him first. Tasha sat down on the sofa with DeMarcus by her side. He used to be my little baby, I couldn't walk into the room without him jumping on my lap. It had been almost a year since we'd seen each other, he probably didn't even remember me. I rubbed my belly, and smiled at his little feet hanging off the couch.

"Do you want a snack or something to eat?" DeMarcus didn't look well at all. Whatever happened to her affected how she took care of him. Usually, he was full of smiles and giggles, but he seemed just a broken down as she did.

"No thank you, we ate before we came." Tasha lied.

"Uh huh, mommy. I'm hungry," he said, starting to cry.

"I'll get you something to eat baby." Any anger I

174

had, disappeared. She was sitting on my couch covered in soars and bruises. Her poor baby didn't look any better than the kids on the feed the children infomercials.

"Fatima, you don't have to do that." She said, as I headed into kitchen.

"Don't worry about it." I gave her a weak smile, and returned with ham sandwiches, chips, cookies, and a pitcher of lemonade for both of them. Tasha was so hungry she bit her tongue. And DeMarcus couldn't stop smiling he was so happy. I felt good knowing he had a full belly. I knew exactly what it felt like to be him. I missed plenty of meals growing up in foster care.

"Thank you so much," Tasha eyes began to water, but no tears fell down. I knew she was really broken, because she never allowed herself to look weak in front of anyone.

"Please. It's nothing. What's going on?"

"I want you to forgive me, Fatima. I shouldn't have done you like that. No man is worth our friendship."

"Tasha, all that's water under the bridge. I have so much going on right now, I'm not even thinking about the past." I lied straight through my teeth. The past was all I thought about. But she didn't need to know that. Even though, I felt bad for her. I still didn't trust her. She showed me who she was. I'd be stupid to forget it."

"Can we start over. I really need a friend right now. You know I don't have anybody else. It's always been me and you. Team Unwanted. Remember?" When were teenagers, we joked about the outcast. The ones nobody wanted. Now it sounded silly hearing her say that. We both were mothers, now. We could never been unwanted. In fact, we'd be needed for along as children lived, at the least. Suddenly, I realized she didn't have the girls with her. I wondered where they were.

"Tasha. Where's Octavia and Nikki? Did you make up with your mom?" She put her head down, and began to cry.

"Fatima. I fucked up. I really fucked up, girl." I got up, and started rubbing her back. In all the years I'd known her, she never cried. At least, not in front of me.

"What happened?"

"Where do I start? Things have been so bad, since we stopped talking. My world just started spinning out of control. For awhile, it was just me and the kids, but then he came back." A chill rushed down my spin, and I moved across the room into Marcus's chair.

"He? Who's he?" I had a good idea who she

meant, but I didn't want to say it.

"Darius," she said, putting her head down. "Darius, came back into my life about six months ago.

I really didn't want to hear anything else. I felt bad life her life wasn't going as planned, but I wasn't going to invite more trouble into mine, trying to help her. "I can't go there, Tasha. I think you should leave."

"Wait. I need a friend. Who else can I talk to? Everyone else doesn't even think he's alive." I knew how she felt. It was hard being tormented by a man in the shadows. She betrayed our friendship, which was unforgivable, but she was literally the only person who could understand my position.

"Go ahead," I said, sitting back down. "You've got fifteen minutes. Marcus will be home soon."

"I got a call from him, saying he needed a ride. I'd been crying for weeks, because they said he was dead on the news. As soon as I heard his voice, all common sense went out the window. I was too relieved to hear he was alive, and okay. Like an idiot, I rushed over to get him. But when I saw him, I was at a lost for words. He looked like the same old Darius, but he was missing a hand, and he was wearing strange clothes. I asked him about it, and he gave me a look that said shut the fuck up. So I did. After, I picked him up, my life was never the same."

I listened as Tasha described what happened. It made perfect sense. Office Moore said they had proof Darius was the man in the fire. Obviously they didn't, because he was still walking around. Maybe they identified his hand. I wanted to know everything about my opponent. In case he decided to show up. I wasn't dumb enough to think I knew who I was dealing with, Darius obviously wasn't the man I thought he was. I couldn't help thinking god was giving me a heads up while she was telling me the story.

"Before I knew it, he was threatening my kids. I didn't want to leave them," she started crying again. "What was I supposed to do? They weren't safe with me. It was like I invited the devil into my home. He took over everything. My house, my car, even my bank account was his. The only time I got away from him was at work. After awhile, I tried to resist. I told him, he needed to get his shit and leave. But he just laughed, and flexed his muscles. Everything is a fucking game to him."

I thought I was going to learn about his intentions, and how they could affect me, Marcus, and the baby. Apparently, she just wanted to get some stuff off her chest, which I didn't have time for. I used to love Tasha like a sister. But I couldn't' have her in my life. It was too much of a risk, and she simply wasn't worth putting Marcus and the baby in danger. "Tasha, I'm sorry you had to go through all that. I really am. But Marcus is going to be home soon. I think you should leave." I stood up, and headed for the door.

"He's a killer," she said, covering DeMarcus ears. "Do you hear me? He's a killer. I need your help."

I was speechless. I sat down, not knowing what to say. Of course, I wasn't surprised. I knew he killed his little brother. I knew he was capable of rape. He assaulted me enough times to know. I couldn't think about what my life would be like, if Marcus didn't find the med pack kept in kitchen cabinet. My baby wouldn't be here. The thought almost brought me to tears. Still, I felt strange having someone confirm my fears. Every time, I tried to talk to Marcus about it, he'd go on a tangent about how he could protect me. He was too busy trying to convince me not to worry. Instead of listening to what I said. The police weren't any help or comfort either. For awhile, I called Officer Moore everyday. Until, he got so tired of me calling, I could only reach his receptionist. Tasha knew more about the new Darius than I did. I was relieved to hear someone agreed with me. Darius was more than a threat. He was a cold blooded killer, capable of anything.

"Do you have proof?"

"Yeah. I have proof. The day I picked him up, I went through his pockets. I was trying to find out, if he was fucking somebody else, but came across something much worse. He had some middle aged white guys wallet in his pants. But that wasn't the worse part. He was carrying a picture of her." She unfolded a newspaper clipping of Emily Bronson. I remember reading an article about her online.

"Did you call the police? I asked, leaning off the edge of my chair.

"Hell nawl, I didn't go to the police. Darius would kill me next. He doesn't know that I'm here. I took a big risk coming to see you. He thinks I'm at work."

"How are you going to get away from him, if you don't involve the police?" I wasn't following her logic. Obviously, my pregnant behind couldn't beat him off her.

"I came to you, because your my sister. I need a place to stay." There was nothing but desperation in her eyes. Sadly, it didn't matter, because I couldn't help her. She made a fool out of me once. I wasn't going to let her doing it again.

"You know I can't do that."

"Fatima. I'm begging you. He's going to kill me, if you don't help. Please," she begged.

I walked to the door, and opened it. It may seem

180

cold, but I wasn't going to put my neck on the line for her. Especially not with a baby on the way. "It's time to go." She carried DeMarcus on her hip, and joined me at the door. I watched Marcus pull into the drive from the doorway.

"You're not going to help me? You know what he's capable of, and your just going to throw me out on the street. What about my baby? Are you really that selfish, Fatima?" True to form, her real self came out. She betrayed my trust, fucked my man, even though he wasn't shit, and now I'm supposed to feel bad because things went wrong.

"Hey. What's going on here?" Marcus looked confused to see Tasha and her baby.

"Nothing, honey. She was just leaving. I'll explain everything to you later." I said, pecking him on the cheek.

"You'll regret not helping me." she said, walking out the door, not knowing I already did.

Chapter 9

Marcus

Finally, I stopped trying, and accepted it was hopeless. Forcing my way into her heart wasn't getting me anywhere. So I decided to give up. She looked so pregnant, it pissed me off. Things weren't supposed to turn out this way. Looking at her swollen with my child made it impossible to ignore the distance between us. Our little princess would be here, any day now. The thought of her being born in such a toxic environment angered me more than anything. Materialistically, Fatima was prepared for birth. We purchased everything imaginable for a new baby and mom. The nursery was set, and ready to go. Fatima even had Shana come over to braid her hair. They only thing left on our to-do-list was getting married. But of course, that didn't go as planned. Instead of being happy, and excited to be with each other for the rest of our lives. We were sitting on my king sized bed throwing blows at each other.

Right before it was time to get in the car, she had to use the bathroom which wasn't bad. But then, five minutes pasted. Then ten. Then twenty. Before long, it was obvious she wasn't coming down. So I cut off the engine, and came back inside. She wasn't downstairs. So I checked the second floor. I found her crying and hyperventilating, like she was marrying a monster. Why be with me? If the thought of marrying me caused stress and anxiety? She claimed, she wasn't having a panic attack because of me. Supposedly, it was because of the night we got attacked. She could have been telling the truth. Unfortunately, I really didn't care. I had enough of the back and forth. Blaming crazy behavior on pregnancy hormones could only go so far.

"Fatima. I can't listen to this shit anymore. I thought we already went over this. We can't make decisions based on what, could happen? It's not practical, and it doesn't make any sense?" I'd been arguing with her for at least a half hour. We were supposed to be getting our marriage license. But suddenly, she got cold feet. I just didn't get it. If she loved me, and wanted to be my wife, what was the problem? Anytime, I tried to get close to her, she brought up my brother. I understood the night of the attack was awful. She would probably never heal from what happened. But seemed like it was becoming an unhealthy obsession. Scratch that, she had been obsessed for awhile.

"I know we have to move on. I want to be with you for the rest of my life. But that doesn't change the facts. He's out there, Marcus. I don't feel comfortable leaving the house, right now. I swear the other day, he was watching me when I went out with the girls. You have to believe me."

"Why the hell would he be watching you?" He's my brother. Remember? That night had nothing to do with you. He was coming after me. The motherfucker is crazy. I told you that. He already killed my brother. He damn near killed my mom. The psychopath probably wanted to take me out, because my dad didn't leave him shit." Her naivety was really started to piss me off. I tried to be patient with her. Especially since she was pregnant. But our little girl was going to be here soon, and I wanted us to be married before she arrived.

"Do you really want to get married like this?"

"Married like what, Fatima? I'm tired of the excuses. Just come out, and say it. You don't love me, and you never have. Anytime I try to get you to be open, and honest, you shut down. And to make matters worse, you walk around like I'm too stupid to notice. I'm tired of trying. It's too exhausting. If you don't want to make this work, we don't have too. I'm out of here.

"Marcus. Wait. Where are you going?" she begged.

"Does it even matter? You don't need me here. You can't like I'm a bitch. You don't believe I can protect you. I might as well be that coat rack sitting in the corner. You have the same amount of faith in my ability to protect you. Besides, when we are together, all you talk about is that night. You don't ask about me, my job, or anything else. You're obsessed with my brother. You can't see past him." She looked like she wanted to say something like usual, but didn't. Why couldn't she just be honest, and tell me what was on her mind.

"You're right. I haven't been fair to you. I just don't know how to get over what happened." I walked around the bed. Sat beside her, then wrapped my arm around her shoulder.

"We can get through this, babe. But you have to open up. When you talk to me, it seems like your holding something back. What is it? Whatever you're going through. We can get through it together." She moved away from me, and leaned up against the headboard.

"Do you promise to stick by my side, no matter what?"

I took a deep breath, and nodded yes.

"We didn't meet organically. We were setup."

I scrunched up my face. What she said didn't make any sense. The first time we met was at my office. She brought DeMarcus in for his appointment. I remembered like it was yesterday. She asked me out, but I turned her down. I didn't think I was ready to get back in the game. She said, her friend Tasha couldn't make it, because she had to go to work. How could that have been a setup? "What do you mean? We met at my office. That wasn't a setup." I said, rubbing the top of my head.

One tear rolled down her cheek, but she quickly wiped it away. "Remember what you said okay?"

"I remember. Just tell me what you've been holding back."

"Tasha wasn't at work. She wanted me to meet you that day."

I let out a nervous laugh, and threw my hands up. "Stop playing girl. You almost gave me a heart attack. So you wanted to meet a doctor. That's not a big deal. You, and every other woman, wants to snag a doctor. That's practically the dream of every single woman."

"Let me get this out. That's not all." She must have been holding on to some serious stuff. Another tear fell, and she swept it away. "DeMarcus is your nephew. His last name is Stewart, because Darius didn't want me to find out he got Tasha pregnant."

"What are you talking about? That boy isn't my family. How would you know if he was, anyway?" Slowly I pieced together the puzzle. "He didn't want you to find out, Tasha was pregnant. You were sleeping with my brother?" She couldn't have meant what she said. All of a sudden, I felt like I was swimming in air. There had to be something I missed.

"I'm sorry, baby. I didn't know how to tell you." Her cheeks were covered in streams.

I was so shocked, I couldn't react. I waited so long to hear the truth, I begged her to put everything on the table. Now I wished, she could take it all back. I scooted to edge of the bed, and crossed my arms. "What else?" I asked, raising my chin.

"Marcus, I'm sorry."

"Shoot."

"I met Darius, four years before we met. I thought I was in love."

I jumped off the bed, I couldn't help myself. How the fuck could she say, she loved him. He was always a monster. He'd been that way since we were kids. Apparently I didn't know her at all. "You loved him. You loved him." Tears were flowing from my eyes now.

"I didn't want to hurt you, Marcus." I could barely understand, over her sobs. "I love you so much. I want us to be together. I didn't know how to tell you. Our relationship wasn't part of the plan.

"The plan! You had a fucking plan. This shit really was a setup." I was screaming now. I felt like my world was crashing down. I thought I loved this woman, when I didn't' even know her.

"It wasn't my plan. It was all Darius. If I didn't to go through with it," she paused. "He forced me. I didn't have a choice."

"He forced you. The thought of being with me was so bad, he had to force you." Every time she opened her mouth, it only got worse.

"No. It's not like that. He was getting blackmailed, and needed half of your inheritance to stay out of jail. He thought, I could talk you out of it."

Fuck. She was supposed to be having my child soon. Now all of this is coming out. Where could we go from here? No wonder she was acting funny. She brought misery back into my life. I went against my instincts, and accepted her advances, now I'm in this fucked up situation.

"Marcus please." She wailed, and grabbed at my shoulder. She tried to lean against me, but I walked away. "If I didn't do what he said, he'd rape me again. I had no other choice, Marcus. Don't do this. I love you."

Suddenly it hit me. "Is Briana even mine?" I asked, tearing my eyes through her. All this time, she watched as I jumped up and down like an idiot. She knew damn well the baby probably wasn't

mine. I couldn't believe it. I probably should have
been more considered about the rape, but I couldn't
care. It was impossible. She ripped my heart apart
like it was piece of rib eye steak. I lost all self
control. The two good things I had to look forward
to were gone. Briana may not be mine. And it didn't
look like we were getting married, anymore. I
couldn't stay, and listen to anymore of what she had
to say. The room was filled with tears, anyway.
Fatima was crying so hard, she couldn't speak. I
took her silence as my answer. God how could this
happen? My baby girl wasn't even mine? I waited
months for this day. I even reminisced about how
happy I was when I married Allison, and had Jamie.
My experience with Fatima wasn't similar in
anyway. The whole scenario smelled like shit. I
thought we'd be celebrating our new union, and
commitment to each other right now. Instead, I
couldn't wait to get away from her. I grabbed my
keys, and jumped in the car. I was ready to drown
my sorrows.

Chapter 10

Fatima

I couldn't breath. My heart felt like it was literally breaking. Every part of my body was rattled with stress. I sucked in air, as best I could. But, I couldn't stop hyperventilating. The worst case scenario just played out in front of my eyes, just like I expected. I didn't want to tell him the truth, but the weight of the lies was eating me up. They were getting harder, and harder, to hold onto. The fact, he kept accusing me of not loving him, because I was distant, made it impossible to continue living a lie.

Marcus left about an hour. The entire time he was gone, I regretted not getting in the car. I did want to marry him. I still wanted to, but the thought of leaving the house, sent me into a downward spiral. I tried to explain why I couldn't go to the courthouse. I knew Darius was out there waiting for an opportunity to strike. There was no denying he was still following me. I didn't have any proof. Besides, the tiny hairs raised on the back of my neck, whenever I decided to leave home. I only left twice, since that night. Once to clear out my apartment. Once to buy baby clothes with my girls, and both times he was there waiting in the thick. It was true. I couldn't prove it was him, who set off my car alarm. But who else could it be? Marcus was at work. And I was with the only other people I dealt with, at the time. I had no doubt in my mind. It was him. Nothing could convince me it wasn't. Of course, I went to my monthly prenatal appointments, too. But other than that, I stayed at home.

Why was Marcus so old fashioned? It shouldn't have mattered, if we got married after Darius was arrested or dead. I wanted to marry him without fear, or worry, looming in the back of my mind. Doing it before then, would cast a negative shadow over our union. I didn't want that. When Briana got older, she wouldn't care, or know the difference, anyway. I couldn't help remembering the hurtful things he said before leaving. Of course, I understood he was angry, and that it would take time for him to process everything I said. Still, it hurt to hear him say he didn't want to be with me anymore.

Briana was kicking, and flipping around the entire time we were arguing. I ignored her increased activity, and tried to stay focus on the conversation at hand. I didn't need him excusing me of avoiding him again. Plus, once I got started, I couldn't stop. Saying it once was bad enough, I figured blurting everything out at once was the best way to go, because I couldn't do it any other way. Now that he was gone, I noticed she wasn't letting up. I placed my hand on my stomach, and realized it was hard as a rock. Should I call Marcus, or head to the hospital alone?

AAH!

The pain was getting stronger. I paced back and forth, trying to walk it off. I didn't want to go in, if it was a false alarm. I read stress could cause contractions, but it usually was a sign of false labor, and not the real deal.

"Ooh, aah, ooh, aah!" It was only getting worse. I reached for the side of my dresser, but missed. Everything on top of it, went crashing onto the floor. Luckily, I fell against the wall, instead of on my back. I needed him to get back home, asap. I dialed his number, but it went straight to voice mail which never happened. I dialed again. Still no response. Obviously, he was still pissed. I jotted down a quick note in case he came back home. Left with no other option, I grabbed my purse and labor bag, before heading for the door. My little girl was coming home sooner than I thought. It didn't matter if I was prepared, or not.

The trip to the hospital was insane. I kept swerving in and out of traffic on the way over. It was a miracle I got there in one piece, and didn't get pulled over. I shut off the engine, in front of labor and delivery, and gripped the steering wheel tightly. I was having the contraction of my life. I heard and felt a strong pop. Before I knew it, the seat of my pants and car were soaked with clear fluid. Dammit. My water broke. I stepped outside with my labor bag and purse thrown over my shoulder. Another contraction was coming on strong. I leaned on the hood of my car, and bared down. She wasn't going to wait for much longer. I grunted into the black sky, and prayed for the strength to make it inside. God. I needed Marcus right now.

"Sorry, girl. I tried to warn you." A voice said from behind me. I felt a prick on the side of my neck, and was out.

*****

The sound of the hood bouncing up and down was excruciating. I reached up, and covered my ears. At the same time, I could feel brightness shining on my face as I slowly opened my eyes. Doing so irritated the sharp pain already cutting through the top of my head. I saw a chain tied from the hood to the latch. It was preventing the trunk from opening or swinging closed. Disgusted by the smell of exhaust fumes, I gagged. Slowly, I gathered my senses. It was still dark outside. It wasn't the sun shining in my face. It was headlights, from the cars in front of me. What happened? Was the first thought to enter my mind. The last thing I

193

remembered was my water breaking. Instinctively, I reached for my belly. Then, I let out a huge sigh of relief. Thank god. She was still there, and moving.

"Aah!"

There went another contraction. I couldn't do anything to relieve the pain. Scrunched inside the back of the trunk, I wasn't able to stretch out, or comfort myself. Hopeless. I began to cry.

"Ssh" I heard someone say from inside the vehicle. "I think she's awake."

I covered my mouth, and did my best to listen. The car went silent, but kept moving. I crossed my fingers, and prayed to god it wouldn't stop.

"I did exactly what you said. Why are you mad?" a female voice asked. I was pretty sure it was Tasha. I would know her voice anywhere.

"I'm mad because I don't need you questioning me shit." Darius said, confirming my worst fear.

"I'm not, baby. As a woman, I know a little bit about these things. I was just making a suggestion."

"A suggestion, huh. Nobody is going to make me miss the birth of my child. Not you, Fatima, Marcus, or any other muthafucker. That's my right as father."

"That's right, baby. I totally agree. I just thought,

we should wait until after she gave birth to kidnap her."

"Bitch are you dumb? I'm not waiting on shit. I deserve to be there, when my daughter enters the world, like I said."

"You're right. Don't let me ruin your moment. I'm so stupid. What I said, didn't make any sense. I don't know what I was thinking."

"And what did I tell you about thinking? I don't keep your ass around to think. All I need you to do, is what I said. You dig? I can do most things with one hand. But other shit, I need your help with. If things get messy tonight. I may need you to jump in."

"What do you mean, you're keeping me around in case things get messy? I don't plan on going no where." Tasha said with an attitude.

"Fatima don't have a lot of kids, like your trifling ass. She may need help delivering the baby. If she does, you may have to jump in." There was no way he was coming near me. I'd be damned, if he touched my baby. I started feeling around the trunk as best I could. I needed to find something to defend myself.

"You want me to help you deliver a baby. Oh hell nawl. I didn't sign up for this shit. Where are we going to do this at? You need a sterile

195

environment to have baby. I've had enough to know. Like you so kindly pointed out."

"Shut the fuck up, bitch. I'm trying to drive. If you don't be quiet. I'll put your ass in the trunk. Like a told you before, I know what I'm doing. I have the perfect spot, picked out. There's only a few miles left, before we get there. We're going to deliver at this abandoned veterinarian center. I ordered scrubs, sterilizer, scissors, and a scalpel. I even bought a clamp to cut the cord. I got this shit, all figured out, I'm telling you. I read Emergency Childbirth from cover to cover. So there ain't shit to worry about."

"Whatever you say. But childbirth don't work like that."

"The more you talk, the more I think I made a mistake. Maybe I don't need to keep your ass around."

"Why do you keep saying that? I don't plan on going no where. You make it sound like you plan on taking me out, or something."

Darius laughed, and a chill shot up my spin. I was crying so hard with my hand over my mouth, it felt like I was having convulsions.

"Did I stutter, bitch. Yeah, I said it. I'm keeping you around. If you keep talking though, I may change my mind. What the fuck are you going to do about it, anyway, bitch."

The car jerked roughly to the side. My head banged against the front of the trunk, not expecting it. Blood dripped over my eye, as the car jumped in and out of lanes. We were no longer on city streets. He turned onto a dirt road, and traveled a few miles, before parking into a forest of trees.

"I told you bitch, I told you." Darius was in a rage. I could hear him banging on the dashboard over Tasha's cries. Out of no where, things got quiet. The door opened, then closed. I could hear him panting, and pacing back and forth in front of the trunk. He walked out of my eye sight, and returned to the car. The next thing I saw was him dragging Tasha body. With a machete as long as my arm. He chopped her up, bit by bit, in front of me. She wasn't my friend, sister, or enemy, anymore. The only thing left was a pile of mangled body parts.

Darius looked between the slit in the trunk. His face was covered in blood, and crazed. I howled so loud, I scared the baby. We both jumped in horror. He fiddled with the padlock, removed the chain, and opened the trunk.

"Hey, Fatty. It's been too long." He wiped the blood off my face with the back of his hand, and dropped her body parts all around me. "It won't be much longer, baby. We're almost there." He kissed me, and replaced the chain.

"No … please no." I whimpered. He got back in the car, and started driving again.

Her corpse was warm, wet, and all over my body. I couldn't take it, anymore. My mind collapsed. I howled and screamed, as loud as I could. What the fuck was I going to do? Somewhere along the way, the contractions stopped, but I felt no relief. They were replaced with a pain too great to describe. I couldn't hope or pray. Reality set in. There would be no rescue team. No one knew I was gone, let alone missing. If they did, it wouldn't matter, because I was kidnapped by a ghost.

Chapter 11

Marcus

"Here's a drink from the lady in the corner." The bartender said, pointing to a woman scantly dressed.

There was no doubting her intentions. Ten of her twenty dollar jeans were in her crotch. And the shirt she wore only covered half her breasts. The rest was on full display. From what I could see, she wasn't my type. Most men would probably find her attractive. But, she was too basic for me. A woman like her was a dime a dozen in the hood, which was one of the many reasons I didn't live there. She was short, thick, and wore a long weave down her back, which wasn't too bad to look at. It obviously wasn't her hair, though. There definitely was an Asian woman running around somewhere bald-headed. I preferred natural beauties. I didn't care for a lot of makeup, and extra shit. Regardless. I nodded my appreciation, and downed the drink. There was no reason to let a good shot go to waste. Especially, when it was what I needed most.

She smiled back, and made her way over. I flagged down the bartender, and motioned for a refill. I was already drunk, but apparently not drunk enough, I really didn't want to talk to her, or anybody else for that matter. Fatima had been running through my mind all night. She called a couple of times earlier, but I turned my phone off, sending her calls straight to voice mail. I hated doing it. But I didn't want to rehash our conversation.

The things she said really fucked me up. I needed to fog up my mind, before I could deal with the situation at home. I had no problem admitting I wasn't man enough to handle what she said. The thought of her with him, made me sick. Rape was one thing. I didn't like that it happened. It was horrible. She shouldn't have been put through that. No one should endure that type of pain. But at least, I could rest easy knowing, she only had feelings for me. Now I knew, she used to love him. The same way, she claims to love me, now.

I just couldn't trust a word she says. What type of woman didn't know who the father of her child is? Yeah. She claimed, he raped her around the time Briana was conceived. But how could I know that was true? She lied to me for over a year, and I didn't even know about it. What other secrets were hiding in the closest? I should have never fell for her. I could kick myself for being so stupid. My instincts told me to keep my head down. Until I was ready to jump back in the dating pool. Now, I was more in love than ever, to a woman that could be pregnant by my psychotic brother.

"Would you like some company, handsome?" She interrupted my thoughts, and slid onto the bar stool next to me.

I tipped my shot glass at her, and downed another shot. "Sure. It's a free country." I said, rubbing my temples with one hand.

"Woman problems?" she grinned, flashing her dimples.

"How'd you guess? I must look pretty pathetic, huh. It didn't take you long to put that together."

"Don't be silly. You don't look pathetic at all. In fact, you're actually kinda cute." She looked a lot better close up. Maybe I rushed to judgment.

I whistled, and motioned for the bartender to fill her up. I might as well enjoy some good conversation while I was here. "Go ahead, and put it on my tab."

"Thanks."

"No problem. It's been awhile since I got a compliment." I said, bitterly.

"Well. I'll have to do something about that. A handsome man like yourself, should never feel unappreciated it. Your wife is a brave woman to let you go out alone." She was laying it on thick. But I didn't care. I needed my ego, and other things stroked.

"What's your name again?" I asked, licking my lips while sneaking a peak of the tightly wrapped mounds spilling out of her shirt. They definitely looked good enough to eat.

"My name is Carla."

"Nice to meet you Carla. I'm Marcus."

"Do you like what you see, Marcus?" She stood up, and pressed her chest against me. "All this could be yours, if you want it to be."

I swallowed the thick lump that formed in my throat. Finally my luck was turning around. "Yeah. You're looking real good tonight, Carla." It had been so long since I busted a nut. I was practically dragging my balls behind me. I wanted to get some pussy so bad, I almost didn't care where it came from.

"Good. Because I like what I see too. Do you mind if I give it a try?"

I nodded my head like a toddler anticipating a cookie. I didn't know what she was going to do next, and I didn't care. My nose was wide open. I wanted to do, whatever she wanted. I just needed some relief.

"Come here, baby." She said, reaching her hands into the front of my pants. I ain't gonna lie. I squealed like a little bitch. The shit was feeling so good. I forgot I was in public.

"My, my, my. Look at you. You're big boy. Aren't you?" I grinned with pride. It was about time, I got some acknowledgment for my gifts. She slipped her warm tongue in my mouth, and began stroking me up and down like a pro. "Do you like that, baby?"

I nodded in pleasure, and she continued.

"I can give you anything you want. What can you give me?" She whispered in my ear. Suddenly, she removed her hand. Zipped up my pants, discreetly. And sat back down on her stool.

My mind was swimming. I didn't want her to stop. Things were just starting to get good.

"I can take care of you. Can you take care of me?" She asked, seductively sucking on the length of her straw.

I realized, what she was asking. She wasn't looking for a casual encounter. There were dollars signs in her eyes. She wanted to get paid. "How much?" I asked, taking another shot. I was mad, hurt, and horny. I'd pay anything for some relief.

"How much am I worth to you baby?" She leaned back in the stool, and started rubbing herself. The bar was so crowded, no one noticed.

"Five hundred dollars." I said proudly, throwing the cash on the bar.

She put the money in between her breast, and

cooed. "Thank you, daddy. Give me one more, and I'll meet you in the bathroom." She strutted across the room with my money in hand.

I quickly paid the tab, and followed her into the men's bathroom. She locked the door behind me, and pulled off her shirt. She had the most perfect breasts I'd ever seen. I reached for them, but she pulled back.

"One more, remember?" she said, removing her pants and underwear.

I dug into my wallet, and paid her fee. I was just happy to be getting some pussy. She shoved her breast in my face. And I filled my mouth with both nipples. I was licking and sucking like a starved beast. It was amazing to hold a woman again. It had been so long, I felt like a born again virgin. She dropped to her knees and took me in her mouth. She was working me from nut to tip. There wasn't a surface she didn't cover. The shit was feeling so good, I shuttered, and nearly exploded. She pulled me out of her mouth, and bent over. I slid inside, and started fucking her from behind. I hate to admit, but I came almost immediately. It felt like the best thirty seconds of my life.

"Thanks," she said, while washing off in the sink. She put her clothes on, and kissed me goodbye.

I looked down at my dick like it committed a

crime. Thanks? She couldn't have said, what I think she said. Could she? Immediately, I sobered up. And it hit. I just had sex with a prostitute in a disgusting public bathroom. What the fuck was wrong with me? I'm supposed to be a doctor, I thought to myself. After she left, I washed up too, and put on my clothes. I needed to get back to my baby. Asap.

When I turned on my phone. I saw I had ten missed calls. Fuck. There had to be something wrong. Fatima never blew my phone up. Guilt suddenly overwhelmed me. What if something was wrong with her, or the baby. I was so angry at myself. I abandoned my responsibilities at home. I had to make it up to her. I grabbed my shit, and jetted towards the house. I kept calling on the way over, but she wasn't picking up the phone. When I got home, I looked for her inside, but she wasn't there. Something was definitely wrong. I did find a note on the refrigerator though. It read:

I'm at the hospital. I couldn't wait any longer.

Love Fatima

I hit the refrigerator so hard. A dent the size of my fist was in it. I really fucked up this time. I couldn't let her have the baby without me. I called labor and delivery to get her room number. To my surprise, they said she wasn't there. How the fuck was that possible? She couldn't have just disappeared. Our wedding rings sat on the counter, and told the full story. She was right. Darius wasn't going to let her go. I should have none better than to leave her alone. That motherfucker had my baby.

Chapter 12

Darius

I'd been waiting for this moment for over nine months. We were finally back together, at last. I was so excited to have Fatima with me again. It was hard keeping my shit together. Of course, everything didn't go as planned. I had to ax that bitch Tasha, before I wanted to. Still, I couldn't regret keeping her around. Since, making her the beneficiary of my life insurance policy was the only way I could afford to make this shit happen. She was so smoked out, and out of her mind, she didn't even realize what she was signing. When I passed her the paperwork. Little did she know, she was the lucky owner of this establishment, a warehouse in the city, and a bank account with five hundred G's in it. I even had her sign a will, making my son the sole beneficiary and trustee, if she died. I couldn't help smiling proudly to myself. My plan was finally coming together.

I hated making Fatima ride in the trunk. I knew that shit had to be uncomfortable as fuck. But what other choice did I have? I couldn't risk her drawing any attention from other drivers on the road. Plus, Tasha fucked up. Since she didn't give her enough morphine to keep her asleep. I told her stupid ass to double the dose. Fatima wasn't supposed to be wake up until we reached our destination. I pulled off the dirt road, and into the abandoned animal clinic parking lot, right outside the city. The large amount of abandoned buildings in Oklahoma, was one of the few things I liked about living here. It made it easy for a rolling stone like me.

Fatima stopped screaming about a half hour ago. I took that as I sign, she was asleep. After the long night she had, I'm sure she needed it. I cut off the engine, and decided to take advantage of the situation by double checking her room, before bringing her in. I wanted to make sure everything was perfect for her, and my baby. I hopped out the car, and ran inside.

Swinging the door open, I was relieved to see everything was just how I left it. The lobby was empty, except for a few old chairs lining the wall. I jogged to the back of the clinic, and scoped out the operating room. The space was updated, and nice. I really did a good job. I bought one of those fancy beds, you can change the settings on. If she got uncomfortable, I could raise or drop the bed with a push of a button. I even had a bassinet set up, right next to the bed, the baby. I couldn't get my hands on one of those expensive machines that monitored blood pressure, and shit. I figured I wouldn't need it anyway. Since back in the day, all they needed was a hot pot of water, some towels, and maybe a piece of wood to bite on. As far as I could tell, I was ahead of the game. She'd be alright. I bet there's a woman giving birth somewhere in the bush right now. Besides, the room was well equipped. There was a sink and left over supplies from when the clinic was open. If her contractions did get too bad, or something went wrong, I had a stack of medications only a few feet away. Given they were for animals.

"She's getting away!" a voice screamed from inside my head. "He's slipping. What the fuck is he waiting for? Your wasting your time trying to help him out." another voice argued. "He's gonna mess this shit up. Right at the end," a third voice interjected.

I slapped the sides of my head, and yelled, "Shut up." I hated when they started saying shit like that. I wasn't slipping. Everything was going according to plan. Except for a few minor details. I pulled the glass dick out of my pocket, and started sucking away. I needed to relax my mind a little bit. My lungs lit up, and my shoulders dropped, before I exhaled deeply. The voices turned down, and started talking quietly amongst themselves. I let out a huge sigh of relief, rolled my neck, and went outside to get Fatima.

"Please … please … Darius. Just let me go. I promise not to say anything," she begged.

209

I ignored her, and started putting Tasha's feet into a black plastic bag. I needed to do something with the body, before I dealt with Fatima. She started screaming again. So I closed the trunk. I didn't need any distractions. There had to be away to get rid of it. I surveyed the grounds, and spotted a metal garbage can behind the building. I'd have to put it in there. I bagged up the rest, and dumped it in the trash can, but I still had another problem. I didn't have any lighter fluid or fuel. Lucky for me, there was plenty of twigs and sticks laying on the ground. "I'd just have to make do," I said out loud to myself. I stirred up the pieces with wood I found laying around, then lit the bin on fire. I knew there was no chance of getting caught, we were miles away from town. I took a few moments, and savored the smell, before bringing Fatima inside her suit.

She was lifeless, her body was limp and stained by blood, carrying her through the threshold was a challenge, but I managed to place her softly on the bed. I brushed away hair covering her eye, and kissed her deeply. Her eyes were a little low, and a bit foggy. But other than that, our kiss was the way I pictured it, in my mind. She didn't resist or even try to fight me. She just laid still on the bed with her eyes closed. I pressed my finger under her noise, and waited. I was relieved to find she was still breathing.

I watched as her stomach faintly raised up and down. I couldn't imagine my life without her. I needed Fatima. I didn't want her. She was the only person who truly knew me. When I looked into her eyes I didn't judgment, dollar signs, or game. I saw love and genuine concern. I needed to see that again. I knew kidnapping her wouldn't work. I had to restore her faith in me, and our relationship. It used to be the only thing she wanted was for us to be a family. I was ready to give her that now. Supporting her during the delivery of our child was the best way I could prove, I changed for the better.

Fatima clutched her stomach, and screamed. "Help. Somebody. Help."

A grabbed her hand, and wiped her forehead with a damp wash cloth I prepared. "Just breathe baby. It's going to be okay. I got everything under control."

"Aah! Aah! I can't take it." She was flailing her hands, and sobbing. "Get off of me. I need a doctor." She wailed, but I knew she didn't mean it.

"Tell me what you need baby. I got everything set." She ignored me, but started pulling at her pants. "Don't worry. I got you." I pulled them, and her panties off. She reached between her legs, and screamed.

"She's ripping me. I can't take it. Oh god. Help me. Help me." When she pulled her hand up, it was

211

covered in blood. I looked between her legs, but didn't know what I was seeing.

"What do you want me to do?" I ran to the medicine cabinet looking for drugs. There had to be something to dull the pain.

"Take me back. Darius. You have to take me back. She's going to die, if you don't."

"I got it." I ran over and tried to stick her with a shot of buprenophine. It was typically used for cats, but I figured, it knocked her out during the drive over. It should definitely take the edge off of the pain.

She slapped the syringe out of my hand. And grabbed at the sides of the rail. "Oh my baby. She's not moving. You killed her. You son of a bitch!" Her mouth was seething with hate. Fatima never yelled, or spoke to me like that. I could feel the rage coming off her.

"Babe, you don't mean that. Calm down. I know you're in a lot of pain."

I couldn't tell if she was laughing or crying. It sounded like she was doing both. "I'm not your fucking babe. You're a psychopath. Why couldn't you just leave us alone?"

"Did you hear that?" a voice snicked from inside. "I did. She called him crazy like everybody else. I told him she wasn't no different." I ripped the medicine cabinet down. They didn't know her like I did. I paced back and forth, trying to calm down.

"I'm sorry, Darius. I didn't mean it." She was reaching between her legs again. "I need your help okay."

I couldn't tell if she was being honest or lying. I wasn't in the mood for games. "You called me a son of bitch. Are you crazy. Don't you ever talk to me like that again." I was heated. I loved Fatima, but she wasn't going to disrespect me. I'd be damned, if she talked to me like I was a bitch.

"Just help me get her out. We don't have time to waste. I can't lose my baby."

"We have to work on our communication skills. If were going to make this work. How are we going to raise a healthy daughter, if there's so much bad blood between us?"

Fatima started laughing or crying again. I couldn't tell which one. Apparently, she still thought I was playing. I'd take care of that shit real quick.

"What are you doing?" she asked rolling from side to side.

I wasn't going to dignify her ass with a response. I picked up the bottle of buprenophine, and three large syringes off the floor. I filled them all up, and jumped on top of her. This bitch was treating me like everybody else. Before she could respond. I stuck all three in her neck, and pushed. She was out like a light. Finally, I could get down to business.

I'm not gonna lie. I was more than disappointed, she hadn't come to her sense yet. I was really hoping to become a family man. But apparently, she needed a little more motivation than I thought. I slapped on a pair of latex gloves, put on my green scrubs, and cleaned the surface of her belly with some damp washed clothes. I watched plenty of episodes of a Baby Story. I knew what I was doing. C-sections looked pretty simple to me. The medical field was just trying to monopolize the market.

First, I wiped across her panty line with some alcohol preps. Then, I made a clean cut from hip to hip. She flinched, and her eyes moved, but she didn't wake up. I put my hands between the cut, and pulled. Blood splattered across my face. Immediately, she howled, and setup in bed. I think she was in shock, because she fell back down just as quick. I pulled my baby out by her butt, and flipped her over. She was stuck. There was no other way to get her out. Delivery was even easier than I expected. She was blue, quiet, and slimy all over. I knew she was supposed to be crying. I laid her across the fold of my arm, and patted her back with my only hand. Mucus came flying out her mouth, and she began to cry.

"We did it, babe. We did it." Fatima was

knocked out, and couldn't here me. I kissed her forehead anyway, and started cleaning off my beautiful daughter with a towel. "It was a long road getting you here, but you finally made it." I kissed my daughter on the cheek, and called Marcus. I was eager to share the good news.

"Fatima?" His voice was hoarse like he'd been crying. I always knew my brother was a bitch.

"Nawl, this ain't Fatima, nigga. You should really get over here, soon though. She's bleeding out. I don't know how long she'll last. But my baby girl is doing excellent."

"I'll kill you motherfucker!"

I hung up the phone, before he could finish his threat. That bitch wasn't about to do shit. I sent the clinic address to his cell phone. He needed to get here soon, if we our little game was going to continue. I smiled to myself, knowing I gave Fatima all the motivation she would need to come back home.

TORN BETWEEN TWO BROTHERS

VOLUME III

Chapter 1

Marcus

I roared down the interstate. Nothing was going to stop me from getting to Fatima. Smacking the steering wheel with one hand, and driving with other, I shifted into fifth gear, and weaved my way through cars. I didn't care if I killed someone along the way. I was on a mission with dire consequences. I would gladly go to prison, or lose my life. I needed to reach my target, no matter what.

"Fuck you! I'm gonna kill you. I'm gonna fucking kill your ass. I swear," I shouted while punching the roof of the car. The taste of salt filled my mouth. Darius was finally successful at breaking me down. I was experiencing a crazed combination of sadness and rage. I couldn't think straight. Since I got his phone call. The tears kept coming. I was an inconsolable mess.

How did I let my pride get in the way? She begged me to stay, but I left anyway. I had no excuse for being so blatantly selfishness. "Lord please, don't take her away from me. I can't live, if she dies," I prayed aloud. "I promise I'll never leave her side again. If you don't take her from me. I

218

swear."

I swerved, and missed a state trooper trying to stop me from speeding ahead. They'd have to do better than that, if they were going to derail my plans. There was no way, a few cops were going to block me from saving the love of my life. A long chain of patrol cars were hot on my trail. They were blaring their sirens, and closing the distance between us. I'm sure we looked like a ghetto set of Christmas lights flying down the interstate. I stuck my head out the window, and saw search lights beaming down on me from the night's sky. They weren't playing. A helicop, and three news stations were tracking my every move.

"This shit was getting out of hand. I had to do something. If I was going to reach her in time."

I stripped off both of my shirts. I threw my navy blue Polo shirt to the side. My white undershirt, I waved outside the window. I wasn't stopping for shit, but I could at least send a peaceful signal. I didn't want any trouble. I just needed to get to her by any means necessary. I veered sharply out of the fast lane, and onto my exit. I was finally out of the city, and onto the dirt road, leading to the abandoned animal clinic.

I checked my rear view mirror, and realized several patrol cars missed the exit. They kept going full speed ahead. The cars near the back of the police chain were able to make it, though. Still, they were a good pace behind me. My brother was the devil personified. He knew how to choose a good place to torture an innocent woman. All the houses out here were inhabitable. It literally was a no mans land, like several pockets in Oklahoma. My headlights revealed the dirt road in front of me, tall oak trees swaying in the breeze lined the street, and vermin scurried in the night.

"I'm coming Fatima. Just hold on. I'm coming. It won't be much longer," I said, assuring myself she was alive.

There could be no other outcome. If she died, I'd be worthless. There was no stopping me from going on a full blown warpath like never seen before. On second thought, that was in the plans anyway. My brother had to die. It was the only way to keep her, and our baby safe. I took a deep breathe, and braced myself. I knew I had to prepare my heart for what I was about to see. Darius told me, I didn't have much time to save her. There was no telling what condition that motherfucker left her in.

The stupid shit I said during our argument early that day, started flooding my thoughts, but I pushed them to the recesses of my mind. Guilt would have to wait. Even worrying about the baby would have to wait, until after she was safe. I couldn't think about what I said, leaving her, or fucking that bitch in the public bathroom, either. Fatima needed me now. And I was going to be there, unlike before.

I tore through the clinic glass door. And sprinted down the hallway, checking every side door along the way. The room at the end of the hall had to be it. I swung the door open, and clutched my stomach at the sight of her.

"Aah! Baby no. No! Look what he did to you," I said, with tears, snot, and spit flying everywhere.

What the fuck did I do? I left her like meat dangling in front of a hyaena. I'm such a piece of shit. I made her pay the consequences for my mistake. How the fuck was she going to survive this shit? He destroyed my baby.

I lifted the throw covering her body. Immediately, I dropped it, and took a step back. Clutching my stomach, I threw up on the floor. She was pieced together like Raggedy Ann. There was jagged and lumpy stitches lining her pelvis from hip to hip.

"I'm gonna kill him. I'm gonna fucking kill him. I'm swear," I said returning to the side of the bed.

I placed my hand on top of her forehead. She was burning up. I checked her pulse, and her wrist flopped down lifelessly. Her pulse was weak, but still there. "Thank you," I said aloud. Fatima looked pale, lethargic, and dehydrated. I lifted her lids, and looked at her pupils. They were uneven, and abnormally dilated. She needed assistance. Asap.

I searched through all the scattered medications on the floor. He obviously went on a rampage, destroying everything in sight, before leaving with the baby. Tears streamed down my face, as I thought about him kidnapping our first child. I killed the negative assault flooding my mind as soon as it came. It would have to wait. Fatima didn't have time to waste.

There was nothing, but animal medications available, but I knew some medication were better than none. So I had to make do with what I had available. Fish antibiotics made by the same pharmacy, I prescribed medications to my kids at the office were laying on top of a pile blue underpads. I crushed five hundred milligrams of clindamyacin between two latex gloves, and put it in her mouth. The bell above the clinic front door rang. I was running out of time. I squirted antibiotic wash, intended for canines, along her incision.

"You're going to make it baby. I got you now. Everything is going to be okay," I said reassuring her, as much as myself.

I took two wash clothes off the counter. I folded one, and scrunched the other. Both, I ran under a stream of cold water. I had to bring her temperature down. The antibiotics would do most of the work by fighting bad microbes and bacteria in her system. But I could still make her more comfortable. I wiped the dried blood off her face, and placed the folded wash cloth on top of her forehead.

I could hear combat boots storming down the hallway, when I was squeezing cold water into her mouth. Fatima was so dehydrated her lips were chapped. And the corners were cracked and bleeding. Light from their flashlights came from underneath the door. I covered her ears in anticipation. I knew they were going blast through like a hurricane.

"Put your hands up, where I can see 'em," a no neck officer yelled.

"Fuck you," I said casually. I ignored him, and continued to squeeze water into her mouth. "She needs medical attention … I'm a doctor … and her husband." I stuttered through the last part. In my heart we were married. Even though, it wasn't legal or official yet. I kicked myself for not being a better man when she needed me the most.

"Bullshit! Step away from the girl. Or I'll shoot." He spat back.

There were officers lining the wall outside the room. I assumed they were organizing to take me out, but I didn't care. I was staying by her side. I refused to make the same mistake again. No one was stopping me from riding with her to the hospital. "She was attacked. I had to speed down here, before she lost too much blood, or suffered irreversible nerve damage. I called an ambulance on the way." As if on cue, I could hear them pulling into the parking lot. "Thank god, they're finally here, baby." I kissed her hand, and waited.

"Get away from her," he shouted while walking up to me with a gun, aimed directly at my head.

"Shoot bitch," I pushed so hard against the barrel, I could feel the imprint on my forehead.

A vein popped out of his forehead, and he pulled the hammer back. I elbowed him in the throat, dropping him to his knees. The gun flew across the room, when he reached for his throat. The officer behind him rushed in, and tazzed me. I drug one foot in front of the other, with volts pulsing through my system. I was still coming for his ass. He turned the voltage up, until I collapsed on the floor. I started flopping around like a fish. Officer No Neck got up, and put his boot across my throat. He aimed, and cocked the gun inches from my face.

My life didn't flash before my eyes. No one's did. There was no review of all the good and bad decisions I made. Real life could never be that simple. That full circle shit displayed on television only happens in the movies. Instead. I thought about the last twenty four hours, and the choices I should have made. Arguing about marriage, and moving on was stupid. Why did I think we could move on with our life? We never could. Not with him alive. He'd fight till the end. Now. So would I. I should have put his ass in the ground when I had the chance. That was my only regret. Leaving him alive was a crime against all mankind, but especially Fatima and the baby. I pierced through him with my eyes. If he wanted fear, he wasn't about to get it from me.

"What the fuck is going on here?" Officer Moore busted through door, yelling. "Marcus get on your feet."

Officer No Neck looked down at me, and slowly removed his foot. I called Moore, right after I got the call from Darius. Paramedics worked around everyone in the room. They moved Fatima on a gurney, and started for the door. "I'm going with her," I said, trying to follow.

"Sir, he assaulted and disarmed an officer. He's under …"

Officer Moore put his hand up. "Let him go."

"Sir …"

"I said, let the man go." Officer No Neck muttered to himself, but didn't come towards me.

"You can arrest him, after she is stabilized," he said, looking at me.

I shook his hand, and hobbled pass him, Officer

No Neck, his sidekick, and the cops stacked in the hallway. Fatima wasn't leaving without me.

Chapter 2

Darius

I stared at the live report on the television screen. This shit was more interesting than any action packed adventure, I'd ever seen. My little brother finally got some nuts. He was giving those pigs hell. I sipped on my forty wrapped in a paper bag, and smacked Marta on the ass. She passed me the pipe stuffed with grade A crystal, and returned to take caring of DeMarcus and the baby in the back of the warehouse.

They had his ass on full display. The news outlets posted his full name, his practice address, where he graduated from medical school, and even listed him as a potential suspect. These crackers literally had me rolling on the floor. A potential suspect? My brother? Hell nawl. He may have upgraded those nuts, but he was still on peanut status. Unlike a real nigga like me. He could never step far outside of the box. He didn't have the imagination or testicular fortitude to do something so creative and bold.

I took charge of the situation. He could never do that. He was always so weak and indecisive. Details and potential outcomes, always got him scrambling and unsure of himself. I on the other had, was a like a skilled lion waiting in the jungle. I'd never wait to pounce on a gazelle. I understand the game. He doesn't. Opportunity has always been a bad bitch. She's flighty as fuck, and waits on no man. She knows she has the best pussy around. So you get no second chances, if you're too busy with your dick in your hand. That's it. You lose. Game over. It's done. Lucky for me, he was holding the shitty end of the stick.

I continued to watch, and laugh out loud at the report on the television screen. These clowns didn't know shit. They couldn't put together a lamp, if I gave them all three pieces. They were reporting straight fiction. I had to give myself a pat on the back for doing such a good job.

Marcus Du Bois was the primary caregiver of DeMarcus Stewart, a four year old boy who had been missing for several weeks. Deputies are unwilling to confirm anything at this moment. However, police did discover a body still burning in the back of the building. They suspect the unknown person is the child's mother Tasha Stewart. Personal information was found a few feet from the body, where Marcus arrived on the scene with the victim. Friends of the family say Tasha disappeared several months ago with her three children. Two of them were turned over to the state, after she dropped them off at a local hospital. Shortly after, she and DeMarcus disappeared.

Unfortunately, the hospital reports the unidentified victim found inside the animal clinic is currently in unstable condition.

Stay tuned for more details. We'll keep you updated. Back to you Bob.

I chucked the remote at wall, and it shattered. How did they ID her so fast? I went through Tasha's purse. I had to double check, but I knew her wallet had to be in there. I made sure to put her purse in the car with me, before burning her body. There was a whole bunch of miscellaneous shit inside, but I couldn't find her wallet. Everything was so chaotic that night, maybe I dropped it.

"You know your ass dropped that shit," I voice chided from inside. "You're going to go to jail, you're going to go to jail," another sang.

"Just the fuck up," I yelled, smacking my head. I heard the baby wailing from in the backroom.

"I need some fucking peace and quiet," I yelled to Marta, "Get the baby." I took another smoke to relax my nerves, then shut off the television. I didn't need anymore more updates. What I needed was to think.

DeMarcus ran from the back, and interrupted my thoughts, "Darius, I'm hungry," he said whining.

"What did I tell you about calling me Darius," I roared. He put his head down, but didn't say

229

anything. I knew his punk ass called me Darius to piss me off.

"Can you get me something to eat." He thought he was slick. He still didn't call me daddy, but I had more important shit to worry about.

"Have Marty get you something to eat," I said, shooing him away.

"She won't."

"The fuck you mean? I drown that bitch in dope. She better get you something to eat."

I was pissed. I could still hear the baby crying. DeMarcus wasn't fed, and the warehouse looked like shit. It wasn't even laid. It only had the basic necessities. I converted the office into a bedroom. The garage floor into a living room, and kept the bathroom as is. Other than the television and couch, we only had clothes and food laying around, but she still couldn't keep the place clean. Matter-of-fact, the only thing the bitch did right was suck my dick, and smoke up my shit. That wasn't our arrangement. I stormed in the bedroom with DeMarcus close behind me.

"What the fuck," This bitch had me all the way fucked up. She was passed out with a syringe in her arm. The baby was crying so much, her face was purple, and she was shaking. Her diaper was full of shit, and piss. The room had empty soda bottles, and wrappers scattered all over the place.

"Marta!"

"Marta!"

Oh, she was going to get up. I shook her by the collar of her shirt. "Get up!"

"Huh," she was disoriented, and stammering. I had enough on my mind. I couldn't waste time worrying about her, doing what the fuck I paid her to do. It was simple. All she had to do was suck and fuck when I said, clean our spot, and take care of the kids. Then, I'd give her as much dope as she wanted. That shit wasn't difficult to understand.

"Get the fuck up, Marta" She was still in a daze. Apparently, this bitch thought I was playing.

"Argh!"

I punched her right in the stomach. If she wasn't go to hold up her in of the deal, I considered that shit stealing.

"Stop! Leave her alone," DeMarcus yelled from behind me. Now he was crying.

"Bitch, what did I tell you, huh?" She muttered something I couldn't understand.

Honestly, I didn't give a fuck what she was talking about. I just kept punching her in the face, over, and over again. All I needed was some cooperation. That was it. Every time, I tried to get a

231

bitch to act right, she turned her back on me, or fought against me. Fatima was playing hard to get, like she didn't want a nigga. Tasha was a low budget bitch that couldn't keep her mouth shut. This bitch couldn't follow basic instructions. I stopped short of knocking her ass out, because she still needed to feed and change the baby. If it wasn't for that, I would have got rid of her ass already.

I met Marta on the street, when I was buying my medicine. She wasn't out there long, before I got a hold of her, or at least that's what she claimed. According to her, she started smoking dope, and selling her ass after a nasty divorce that happened three months ago. I believed her, because she wasn't all sucked up, and used looking like a lot of bitches fucking for rocks. I decided to give her an opportunity to get high without being in danger, but she couldn't keep her word like the rest of these worthless bitches, today.

I rested against the wall, and caught my breath. Marta sat up, and staggered to the crib. She started changing and feeding the baby, like she should have been doing in the first place. DeMarcus wiped his tears, and walked up to me.

"Where's my momma?" he asked with a scowl on his face.

"Go play, little nigga. I'm busy."

"Where's my momma?" he said louder. I

couldn't help it. I laughed. This nigga was trying to punk me.

"If you don't shut the fuck up, I'm gonna beat your ass."

He wiped the tears off his cheeks with the back of his hand. "When is she coming back? I want to go home."

I had to respect his spirit. He got his courage from me. I handed him a bag of Doritos, and a soda, and told him to go eat, but he didn't walk away. "DeMarcus. Go sit the fuck down, and eat. I'm not playing with your ass."

He bawled up his fist, and started swinging on me. I laughed so hard, tears where streaming down my face. He was really trying to fuck me up. I covered my head, and pretended he was putting in some serious work. My laughter only pissed him off more.

"I know what you did. I saw you. I saw everything. It's your fault my sisters are gone. You made them leave." I grabbed him by the shoulders, and looked him square in the eye.

"You need to chill the fuck out. That shit's over now. You'll be alright. You're just like your old man."

"I'm nothing like you. Don't say that! I hate you. I wish you were dead. Where's my mom? You took her away from me. You said, she was coming back. You lied."

"So what, I lied, nigga. You ain't about to do shit," I chided.

"Fatty hates you too. Just like I do. She'll never be with you again. My momma told me," that bitch talked about me to my son. Now he thought he could humiliate, or talking about my relationship with my woman.

I grabbed him by his throat, and raised him off the ground. His little head looked like it was going to pop off. Marta stepped towards me with the baby in her hand, but I gave her a deadly look, and she stepped back. I dropped him on the floor, and he broke down crying. His ass should have thought twice about talking shit. Because I wasn't done yet. I pulled off my belted, and started swinging wildly. I covered every inch of his body. Marta, the baby, and he was crying. They all understood who was in charge.

"Marta, make sure he gets something to eat, and goes to bed." I looped my belt, and left the room.

Chapter 3

Fatima

Berenice kept blocking my way with her three hundred pound body. Her short ashy blonde hair, swung in and out of my nostrils. Since, she wouldn't let me pass, and was shaking her head like an excited preschooler. Even though, she was a middle aged woman with a tree trunk frame.

"Oh I'm so excited," she said clapping her hands. "I saw you on television you're a movie star. Can I have your autograph?" she thrusted her note pad and pen in my face. I ignored her, and pivoted towards the opposite end of the room.

Weekly, I was forced to come out of my dorm to interact with the other patients at Saint Mary's Behavioral Ward. I loathed coming out. It was the worst part about being committed. I didn't mind the food. It wasn't great. But it was edible. The staff didn't bother me, and I didn't bother them. So that wasn't that bad either. It was the other patients that drove me up the wall. I just wanted to stay in my room, and read without being disturbed.

I sat in a chair, next to the vending machine. There was a flat screen television on the wall, other residents were watching. I couldn't say what was on the screen, because ever since Darius stole my baby, and attacked me, I avoided television all together. I needed to block everything out. From what I could gather, my story was every. Instead, I watched the clock. It was a quarter till three. I had fifteen minutes before my appointment with Dr. West. I could see Berenice titer tottering over to me. I sunk down in my chair, and covered my face.

"Pretty pretty please. Can I get your autograph, Mrs. Movie Star Lady." I wanted to rip the pen out of her hand, and jam it down ear drum. I chose to take a deep breath. I couldn't do that. She obviously was crazy and special, which was a dangerous combination, in my opinion. Mr. Price, a tall Baluu looking man, walked up, and lead her across the room by the elbow. "Thank god," I said aloud. I looked up, and saw it was three o'clock.

"It's been six weeks since the attack, how are you feeling?" Dr. West asked, but I didn't answer.

He sat across from me at his desk, while I reclined on the leather sofa in his office. It was nice getting out of my dorm room for awhile, without being around the other patients. His office was a welcomed change in scenery. He wasn't too bad, either. He seemed nice enough. I didn't find him threatening at all. He was middle aged, white, and appeared to like his job. This was our sixth session together. The first few times, he visited me in my recovery room downstairs, after my surgery. He

236

was still trying so hard to help me. Even though, I hadn't said anything to him before, and didn't plan on saying anything now.

"Fatima. We can sit here, if you like. But I'd rather help you move forward. We can start wherever you feel comfortable. I know you've been through a lot." I couldn't help laughing.

He jotted something down on his note pad, which only amused me more. I didn't care, if I died inside this place. At least, I didn't have to worry about being attacked, betrayed, or left behind. I was tired of fighting just to lose in the end, anyway. It actually felt like home being here. It was very similar to the shelters and girls homes, I grew up in as a child. Everyone was crazy in there too. We just weren't certifiable. I bet the majority of us were now, though. The thought made me giggle, I'm not gonna lie.

"Staff members are concerned you're not making any progress. They say you haven't been interacting with them, or other residents here. Why is that?"

What the hell would be the point? There was no way anyone could understand me. I was already an odd duck, because I didn't have any family. When you add being raped by your fiance, falling in love with his brother, getting pregnant by one of them, but not knowing which one, being betrayed by your closest friend, and confessing to the man you love, only to get left by him, before his insane brother kidnaps and literally rips your baby out of your body, there was nothing to discuss. The shit was horrendous and unconscionable. So why even try to figure it out? He could never understand the hell I went through. I could careless how many licenses, or degree he had hanging on the wall.

When I woke up in the hospital without my child. I literally lost my mind. I decided to shut down that day. I hadn't said a word to anyone since what happened to me in the clinic. That was their reason for throwing me in this place. I wasn't opening up to anyone, or anything, again. It wasn't worth the risk of getting hurt.

"I understand Marcus has been calling you everyday, still. Why don't you want to hear from him?"

He asked another obvious question, I'm sure he knew the answer to. When I gained consciousness, after my surgery, Marcus wasn't there. The nurses kept telling me he called everyday while I was recovering. How convenient. He called when I was unconscious, but disappeared when I was awake. If what they said was true, that would just be my luck. Regardless. The fact he called, instead of showing his face, told me how much he cared. At first, I believed what he said during our argument was out of hurt, and anger. Especially, when they told me he got arrested after I was stabilized. Since, he wouldn't leave after the police arrived. According to the nurses, half the gifts and flowers suffocating my room where from him. The other half were condolences from considered citizens. It still didn't matter to me, though. I would have rather had him with me at the time. A huge part of me was relieved he wasn't there. Not seeing his face allowed met to forget about him, Darius, Tasha, and the baby. Eventually, I got numb, and stopped hoping he'd show up after awhile.

I hated looking around my hospital room. It felt like I was participating in my own funeral, minus the guests that loved me. All the flowers and cards were so morbid to me. No one I knew was there for me when I needed them most. Shana, Denise, and Trina were sheisty bitches. None of them hos showed up, which made me miss Tasha more than I already did. Did she fuck me over. Yes. Did she fuck the man I loved at the time. She sure did. But I knew, SWAT couldn't hold her back from seeing me in the hospital, if she were alive. One of my biggest regrets was not helping her that day. I replayed our conversation over, and over again in my head. She was wrong, and a piece of shit for drugging me. But I knew Darius was capable of doing anything, in order to get what he wanted. He couldn't have threatened her or her kids. Who knows?

I didn't know why my so called girls didn't show

up. Maybe they couldn't handle seeing me in such bad shape. Or maybe the bitches simply didn't care. Truth be told, I didn't give a fuck anymore, anyway. I no longer wanted love, or people in my life. For the first time ever, I didn't give a fuck about having a family, which was a good thing as far as I was concerned. I understood most people couldn't relate to my situation. It was a lot to handle, even for me. To be honest, I did think I could count on Marcus. Obviously I was stupid to think that.

When my doctor asked questions like "how are you feeling," I couldn't help thinking he wasn't qualified to ask me any questions at all, no matter how much he wanted to help me. Obviously, I was feeling alone. Demoralized. And tired of trying to standup, just to get knocked down again. It took more than four weeks to recover from my reconstructive c-section. After Darius butchered me. I still wasn't a hundred percent healed. My incision sight was extremely sore. I still had difficulty getting around. But at least I wasn't strapped to a bed, unable to go to the bathroom by myself like before. I used all my strength to recover physically. I didn't have anything left for my mind. I just wanted to live safely and quietly, by myself.

I could see Dr. West writing at lightening speed on his note pad out of the corner of my eye. I figured the crazier, I seemed the better. At least, I wouldn't have to deal with the hot pile of shit, also known as my life. He put his note pad on his desk, pulled his chair in front of me, and sat down.

"Look. I'm gonna cut the shit, and be real with you right now. Okay?" He hooked his glasses on his shirt collar, and looked deeply into my eyes.

"Life can be a bitch. Believe me, I've been through a lot of shit, too. I'm not going to lie, and tell you I understand how you feel. But I get why you're refusing to cooperate with me. The police told me how you held onto your friends wallet, when you were trapped in the trunk with her body. It takes a strong person to think about someone else, when your own life is in danger. Who knows if they could have identified her body without you leaving that vital piece of evidence." His words pierced a tiny whole through my armor. I hadn't thought about the details of what happened that night. It was too painful.

"I want you to know, I won't discharge you until you're ready. You can speak to me without fear of getting turned out on the street. You're young with a full life ahead of you. You have to believe, you can turn this ship around. Just think about it, okay." He gave me a weak smile, and returned to his desk.

"Thank you," I said, wiping a tear from my eye. It was good to hear reassuring words. I wasn't ready to face my demons yet. Darius in particular. But knowing I didn't have to worry about coming across

him, relieved a lot of my stress. I left his office
feeling better than when I arrived which was a good
change.

Chapter 4

Marcus

"Get up."

A dieseled out looking dude said, throwing his tray down next to mine. He appeared to out weigh me by a hundred pounds, give or take a few. I could tell he was about six inches taller than me too. Even though, I was sitting down on the bench, and he was standing up. I couldn't say, I came across too many men larger than myself. It wasn't surprising to find one inside the county jail, though. The correction officers weren't fazed. They continued chopping it up with other officers, and inmates. It was there would be no rescue team coming my way.

I slowly opened up my chocolate milk, and downed it like I didn't hear anything. Fuck him. I wasn't getting up. If I wanted to get out of jail soon, I had to keep my nose clean though. So I wasn't trying to fight, because I didn't need time added to my sentence, if I was convicted. I still wasn't going to act like a bitch though. My court date was around the corner. According to my lawyer, I'd be free in a matter of days. My status as a doctor, and reputation as a productive and upstanding citizen was working in my favor. Plus, he was trying to get the district attorney to drop all charges due to exceptional circumstances. If I had to go round and round with this fool. It could stop that from happening. Obviously, I didn't want that.

"You think I'm playing with you nigga?" he spat on my back.

I put down my toast, clinched my fists, and stood up. This fool wasn't gonna back down. I flexed, and stepped into his bubble. "What's the problem?" There was no one else at the table. His name definitely wasn't on the seat. He just wanted to try me.

"Hey, what's up baby?" A man with my build and tone, exchanged a handshake with dude, and intervened. I unclenched my fists, and stepped back.

"What up," he responded staring me down, but pushed off.

"Everything good here?"

"Yeah."

The big dude sat at another table. I returned to my seat, and started eating.

"I'm Butter."

The guy who intervened extended his hand, and sat beside me. I shook it, and got up with my tray. I didn't feel like talking, or making new friends, especially not here.

"Wait up." He followed behind me, and dumped his tray too.

I ignored him, and strolled onto the yard. He was only a step behind me.

"I don't get a thank you? What's good?" He threw his hands up in anticipation of an apology.

"Thank you."

"Oh, that's cold blooded." He laughed, and joined me on the outside bleachers.

"No disrespect. I prefer to stick to myself."

"Stick to yourself, if you want to. I'm not stopping you. I was just trying to help a nigga out. This ain't Oz my nigga. Ain't nobody trying to shank you, or nothing." He started to get up. Maybe I was doing the most. I just had a lot on my mind, and didn't need any more trouble.

"You're good." I motioned for him to sit down.

"That's what's up. We're cellmates anyway. You couldn't avoid me, if you wanted to." He laughed.

"Is that right. What happened to Mike?"

"He left this morning. I'm jealous like a muthafucker. I wish it was me."

"Me too."

"I hear you my nig. I hear you."

245

I hated that word more than anything. Being inside, only made me hate it more. Seeing my own people talk to each other like trash really got under my skin. I couldn't believe, I ended up with the worst of society. I never thought, I'd find myself sitting in jail. That was why I spent all those nights studying, and doing my residency. I was trying to avoid becoming the black male stereotype, people loved to believe. The last year was nothing like I expected. Hell, the last few hours weren't.

I wanted to run through the metal gates guarded the jail, into my car, and straight for Fatima. She hadn't returned any of my phone calls or letters. The shit was really starting to get to me. I spoke to everyone at the hospital. None of them could convince her to get on the phone. In my heart, I knew she was hurting, and having a hard time. I just thought she would be open to talk to me, by now.

The day took forever to pass. I could only watch so many scuffles over fun sized potato chips, and juice boxes. I felt like I was in the second grade again. By the time, it was time to lock up, and go to sleep, I was depressed and exhausted. Butter had the top bunk, and I had the bottom. He wasn't to bad to deal with. In fact, it was interesting to listen to him talk about his life growing up in the corrections system.

He told me stories about doing time for a set he

joined as a teenager. You'd think a forty something year old man would have more to be proud of, but he didn't. His face lit up with pride as he reminisced about slinging. He actually considered himself a business man, because he sold eight balls to children and mothers on sleazy street corners. It was disgusting. But it was obvious he had no shame. The funny thing was none of his homies remembered his ass when he got locked up. He was actually surprised. He didn't get any calls from them, or family and friends. But it didn't seem to bother him too much. In fact, he seemed happy. It was obvious, he belonged in jail.

The hallway lights went out, and I climbed into bed with my note pad, and pen. I was ready to get some much needed sleep, but Butter kept talking to me all day. So I had to use the moment of silence to pen another letter to Fatima. Unfortunately, I felt him jump out of bed. How could he possibly having anything else to say? He hadn't closed his mouth all day. I slipped the pen and behind my ear, and pretended to be asleep.

"Mark. You up?"

I ignored him.

He cleared his throat, and said it louder. "Mark. You up?"

I ignored him, again.

"Nigga you hear me. I can see your eyes shaking. Get up. Nigga. Damn." He shook my shoulder this time.

"What do you want? I'm tired."

"I need you to handle something for me." He tugged at the front of his pants.

This fool had me fucked up. If he meant, what I thought he meant. "Handle something for you. What the fuck are you talking about?"

"Look, this is just how shit rolls, inside." He said, grabbing himself again.

"Fuck you. I ain't handling shit." My tongue dried out, and my pulse began to race. Beads of sweat starting to run down my face. I tried to keep a cool head, but I knew I looked nervous. Somehow, I managed to do my time peacefully, with little to no issues so far. Now my worse nightmare was coming true. If this wasn't some Oz type shit, I didn't know what was.

"You gonna handle my shit whether you like it or not. You owe me, my nigga. We can do it nice, or rough. Personally, I like it both ways."

He pulled down his pants, and revealed himself. He was dead serious. I swallowed the large lump in my throat, and got off my bunk. I had to take care of business. He showed me his hand. There was a shank it. He was prepared to fight. I stroked his shoulder to relax him. And he put the shank on top of his bed. I was scared to death. I ain't gonna lie. I didn't know what the fuck to do. He had me cornered. I peaked over his shoulder, and saw the guards standing way down the hallway.

"Don't get any ideas. You'd be bleeding to death by the time they got here."

I knew his was right. They weren't going to put there life on the line for mine. The inmates ran the jail, not them. Their blood ran just as easily as ours. I got down on my knees. I had no other choice. Shit was going down either way.

"Yeah. Handle that shit like a good boy. I ain't gonna tell nobody." He laughed.

I rubbed on his thighs, and looked up at him. I couldn't beat him, one on one. Sure, I was just as tall and strong as him, but he'd been fighting all his life. Instantly, I realized that was the point of telling all those stories earlier today. He was letting me know, he knew the game. He let out a sigh, and rubbed on my head. He pulled my mouth closer to him, and I put in work.

Aagh!

He started swinging, but I got the jump. I slipped the pen out of my pocket and stabbed him, over and over again. Blood was spilling from the main artery lining his groan. He was bleeding out, fast. I could see the guards running toward our cell from the other end of the hall. I was knotting him up, and digging my hands into the gap I created above his thigh. The audacity of this nigga. Yeah, I called his ass a nigga, cause that was exactly what he was. I found a new appreciation for the word.

"He attacked me," he cried, holding himself. The guards threw me onto the floor, and radioed, I was going to seg which was fine with me. I'd be damned, if a nigga thought he was gonna turn me out. I'd just have to deal with the consequences. I was more than happy to go to segmented administration with my cheeks, and manhood completely in tact.

*****

"We have to stop meeting like this." Officer Moore said, shaking his head.

I was isolated, and kept behind a steel door. The correctional institution considered me a high risk inmate. Nothing could've been further from the truth. As long as, people kept their distance, I was good. He spoke to me through the tiny window, at the top of the door. Somehow, he got word of my situation.

"We don't have to meet at all," I said. Why the hell, he was even here? I didn't get it. I was grown enough to understand what I did. I didn't need a man, who has never been in my situation slapping me on the wrist.

"Don't get lippy with me. I'm here to stop you from destroying your life." He was genuinely pissed. He face turned different shades of red, faster than I thought possible.

"Excuse me, I didn't know you cared." I laughed, not caring for the conversation.

"Listen to me, you fucking idiot. I put my neck on the line, for you. James called my office, and told me about your situation. I personally took time out of my day, to speak to the district attorney, who happens to play golf every week with my father in law. I was able to convince him to drop the charges. But then you turned around and did this stupid shit."

My face dropped. I didn't know what to say. I really felt like an idiot. "Thanks anyway," I muttered.

"Luckily, I was able to still get you out of here. The DNA results came back from Tasha Stewart. It matched the Good Wife Killer case files. I'm sorry we didn't believe you and Fatima. We should have."

I didn't feel like I should. Why wasn't I jumping up and down like a won the lottery.

"You don't have anything to say?"

"That's good news I guess."

"What the hell are you talking about? That's the news of the century. We can finally nail that fucker." He was looking at me like a second head was growing out of the side of my neck. "Oh forget. You're getting discharged tomorrow morning. Keep your ass out of trouble. I'm not helping you anymore."

Officer Moore walked down the hallway shaking his head. He wanted something I couldn't give him. In my opinion, it wasn't good news Darius was on their radar. I wanted to kill him, myself. Jail and lethal injection were both too good for him. The only thing he deserved was death by my hands. I looked forward to personally delivering his sentence.

Chapter 5

Fatima

"What is he doing here?" I asked, pointing to Marcus. My therapist completely betrayed me. I told him how much I needed to be alone right now, but he invited him to my session anyway.

"Fatima. Believe me. It's for the best. Everyone needs a support system to get back on their feet. Who better than Marcus to support you through your recovery? He's the person that can understand your situation."

He couldn't be serious. Marcus was sitting in the trunk with me, and Tasha's broken down body. I don't think so. I was in there suffering alone. No one else was in labor, laying beside me. He was gone somewhere, blocking my calls, because he couldn't handle my past mistakes. I wouldn't say he was able to understand my situation at all. If he could, I wouldn't have been alone when Darius got me.

Marcus sat across the room with his head down. He was visibly uncomfortable. I wondered, if he even wanted to be here. His body language was closed off, and unsure. He didn't even try to make eye contact with me when I came into the room.

Apparently, he knew I was pissed.

"You lied Dr. West. We had an agreement. You promised to take things slow, until I was ready."

"I didn't lie to you, Fatima. You've been making significant progress. Staff tells me, you've been interacting more, and showing steady signs of growth. I want to encourage you, and keep things moving in a positive direction by nudging you outside of your comfort zone. I promise, I'm doing this because I know, it will help you."

I folded my arms, and stared across the room. I wasn't going to win this battle. So I stopped trying.

"Marcus. Do you have anything you want to say?" He gave him an encourage smile. I did my best to counteract it by twisting up my face. Whenever he wanted to say, I wasn't going to make it easy. He certainly, didn't make life easier for me, or my daughter that day.

He cleared his throat, and sat up straight. "I hate the circumstances. But it's good seeing you again. You look beautiful as usual." His eyes were soft, and pleading. I didn't want to hear anything he had to say. It was too little, too late. At this point, nothing in the past mattered to me anymore.

"Can we cut to the chase please? I don't want to do this. Trying to get over what happened was bad enough without you dragging me back to the past."

"Fatima. I know this is hard for you. But Marcus is a survivor as well. You two can be a great strength to each other. I don't want you guys to rehash the bad things that have happened. Instead, I need you to take the good out of the situation. So you can better move forward."

"Take the good out of the situation, huh?" I laughed. He couldn't be serious? There was no good, in the situation. Unlike, everyone else, I saw the full picture, including the frame. Marcus could paint himself as a victim while trying to find the right angle, but it wouldn't change anything. The reality of the situation was he avoided me when I was in labor, and needing his help. As far as I was concerned, he was only a lick better than Darius.

"Maybe this wasn't a good idea," Marcus stood up to leave.

"No. Please sit down. You're doing great. I know how much it took for you to come here." Marcus sat back down, and Dr. West directed his attention toward me. "This has to happen. Whether you realize it or not, things aren't going to get better by avoiding the situation."

"Fine. I'll participate. He needs to know how I feel anyway." I sat on the edge of my chair, and peered across the room. "The truth is I loved you, Marcus. I really did. I trusted you. I thought you'd protect me, and that we'd be together, after my baby was born. Note. I said, my baby, because you made it clear, she wasn't yours. Not that she's already gone, and there's nothing to show for my life, I don't want to see you, or even hear your name. Do you know what was happening to me, when you were blocking my calls? Do you?" I was yelling now. They wanted to hear the truth. So I was going to give it to them.

"That's good Fatima. Let it out. Marcus, what do you have to say."

"I'm sorry. What else can I say? I'm sorry, I said those awful things to you. I'm sorry, I didn't answer my phone. I'm sorry I wasn't there for you when you woke up. I'm sorry for everything you've been through. If there was anything, I could do to change the way things turned out, I would in a second." He eyes welled up with tears.

To my surprise, he wasn't trying to defend himself, or make up excuses. I felt so dumb. I was speechless.

"Good. I'm glad you were both able to get everything on the table. Is there anything else, either of you want to say?"

Marcus spoke up. "I want you to know, I still love you. I don't care about what has happened in the past. If you give me a chance, I'll prove how much I love you, and our daughter. I'm willing to wait, if you want me to."

After all the horrible things I said to him, he still wanted to be with me. I couldn't wrap my mind around what he said. So I stayed quiet.

"Did you hear what he said, Fatima? Do you want to give your relationship, or friendship, another shot? It seems like there's still a lot of potential there."

My heart wouldn't buy the lies my mind was selling. I could yell, and scream all I wanted, but I still loved him. Seeing his face again, made me think of our daughter, and the life we could have had. "I don't know, if I can do that right now." I told the truth. Even though, I missed him, I wasn't ready to be vulnerable again. I still felt like I was walking around with no skin on.

"Take all the time you need, babe." He sighed, and flashed a big smile. I grinned too. I think we both felt a huge weight, lifted off our shoulders.

"Before we end our session, Marcus had some news he needed to share with you." Dr. West motioned his way.

"Oh yeah, I almost forgot. I was so happy to see you again. It slipped my mind. Officer Moore was able to match the DNA results found at clinic with the victims of the Good Wife Killer. They're finally updating his records. Darius is a wanted man now. And not just by the state." His face changed when he said his name. It was obvious he hated him, as much as, I did.

"See Fatima. Even in a desperate situation, you were able to help strangers you've never met. The family and friends of those victims are enormously grateful. Think about all the woman, who won't come across Darius when he's found. You still have a lot of strength, and life left. You just have to find it again."

"I'm glad, they're looking for him now. I'll sleep a little easier tonight."

I really noticed Marcus for the first time during the visit. He didn't look like himself. His eyes were low, and tired. It appeared he picked up a few crows feet since the last time, I saw him. Maybe Dr. West was right. He didn't experience the same things I did, but he certainly was a victim. The thick scar wrapped around the front of his neck, wouldn't let me deny the pain he'd been through. He must have seen the pain, and softness in my eyes, because he walked over to the couch, and hugged me. He held on to me so tight. I thought I was going to burst. It felt so good to be in his embrace again. Instantly, I remembered all the good times we shared.

"I shouldn't have attacked you. I'm sorry." Before I could stop the words from leaving my lips, they were already out there. Marcus successfully disarmed my defenses by being kind and understanding, regardless of the blows I sent his way. Now I felt embarrassed, because I planned on never speaking to him again. My behavior was unreasonable. It wasn't hard to tell who the immature, and unforgiving person was in the room.

"None of that matters now. I'm just glad to see you." I looked into his deep brown eyes, and began to cry. Why didn't we fall in love, and live happily ever after like the stories I read as a child. He was such a good man. We deserved a fairy tale ending. He wiped the tears from my cheeks, and kissed them. "I want you to know, I'm going to get our Briana back. No matter what happens, I swear. I know she's out there. I can feel it. Darius wouldn't hurt her anyway. Because she is his most valuable chest piece." He whispered, "I'm gonna get him, before the police. I promise you'll sleep peaceful every night."

"Marcus …" Even though, the tension in the room disappeared. He placed a finger over my lips. I could only assume, he felt my apprehension. I was going to tell him don't bother looking for Darius. I was finally ready to accept my situation. It was nice seeing him, and getting closure, but I still wasn't ready to confront Darius having our daughter.

Chapter 6

Marcus

I debated whether or not to go inside. My mom's doctor said, she was having another manic episode, and kept calling for my father, Darius. Since, I was the only living relative she had left, besides my brother of course, the responsibility fell squarely on my shoulders. I hadn't seen her in over a year. And honestly, I wasn't looking forward to seeing her now. Things weren't bad between us. It was just too difficult to see her in such bad shape. She didn't remember me half the time, and when she did, she never had anything positive to say. It was like her mind only kept record of the traumatic, and horrible events that occurred in her life. It was simply too depressing to deal with.

I decided to man up, and go inside, anyway. I pressed the call box, and waited, "Yes?" a voice called over the intercom.

"I'm here to see my mother "Lu Ann Du Bois," the intercom buzzed, and the gates opened. I made sure to put her in the best home money could buy. If she was too ill to live with me, I at least wanted her well taken care of elsewhere. I drove pass the stone lions guarding the entrance gates, and made my way up the wrap around driveway. The attendee took my keys, and parked the car, before I entered the nursing home double doors.

"Can I help you?" I small blonde asked from the nurses station.

"Yes, I'm Marcus Du Bois." Dr. Cashing called me earlier today. She suggested, I come visit my mom Lu Ann, because she's been having regular episodes lately.

"Oh you're hear to see Lu Ann. Bless your heart," she said, giving me a sympathetic smile. "Come this way sir." She lead me to the back of the facility. It was beautiful outside. There was a nice waterfall right through the court yard entrance. It ran into a pond full of water lilies, and other floating plants. As we made our way to my mom, we passed an assortment of exotic perennials, garden stones, and humming birds feeding from their dishes. It was like stepping into Snow White's backyard out here.

"There's she is," the lady said, pointing to my mother sitting on a cement bench feeding some squirrels.

"Thanks," I replied. She looked as beautiful as I remembered. She was still tall and slender. Her curly salt and pepper hair was wrapped into her signature french roll, she always pinned with a silver dragonfly comb my grandmother gave her.

261

"Hi my mom," I said, sitting beside her.

"Oh Darius. They finally called you." She threw her arms around me, and held on tight. "I thought you'd never come."

"I'm not Darius. I'm Marcus mom. How have you been doing?"

"Don't be silly, Darius. I know who you are. Did Sally get those cookies, I made for the church bake sale? Me and Marcus stayed up making them all night. He's such a good boy." She bent down, and fed the squirrels as she talked. A huge grin swept over her face.

It broke my heart to see her so happily confused. I didn't know what to say.

"I want to thank you for being so good to me. You didn't have to stay with me, after what I told you."

What was she talking about? I'm sure I didn't know all my parent's business, but I wasn't aware of any major secrets. I wanted to know more information.

My mom stopped feeding the squirrels, and came to sit beside me. She grabbed both my hands, placed them in her lap, and looked deeply into my eyes. "You didn't have to accept Darius as your son. But you did, because you're such a good man. After what my daddy did to me, I thought nobody would want me. I appreciate you taking me in." She patted the top of my hand when she spoke. It was obviously difficult for her to say.

After my visit with Fatima, I couldn't stop thinking about my mom. Looking back, she really had her shit together, especially considering her background. At least, she had it together before Eric passed away. She seemed more impressive now, because I didn't know my grandfather assaulted her.

She was an excellent mother, despite her upbringing. Every morning, she would put me and Darius on the school bus with Eddie wrapped tightly around her waist. We would get bum-rushed with kisses and hugs before she sent us off. Of course, other kids on the bus made fun of me for being a momma's boy. But I didn't care. To me, she was the most beautiful woman in the world. Her beauty was only out-shined by her generous heart, and love for me. Fatima reminded me of her, so much. Before she was attacked. It was one of the many reasons I fell in love with her. Unfortunately, they were more similar than I would like for them to be. They both withdrew, when life got too rough.

As a kid, my little league coaches would volunteer to take me home after practice. Just so they could find a reason to speak to her. They knew she was married, but that didn't stop them. They even tried to buy her affections by spoiling me, and my brothers, with candy and toys. She never accepted their advances or gifts. Somehow, she managed to deny them without bruising their egos, or causing bad blood. She really was a class act. You'd think all the men stiffing around would keep my dad on his toes, but it didn't. Maybe her huge revelation about my granddad, fathering Darius was the reason for his coldness. Growing up, he seemed too arrogant to care about any of us, but especially Darius, and my mom. He never appreciated the fact he had a good woman waiting for him at home. I'll never understand why they stayed married so long. Neither of them seemed happy. How they lasted until his death would always remain a mystery to me. Most of the time, he was too busy to be bothered with us, because he was chasing after half the congregation. He hardly noticed my siblings, or mom. I guess her survivor's guilt stopped her from ever straying, or divorcing him.

"You know he is just like him," she said, starring off into the distance.

"Little Darius?" I asked, making sure I was following.

"Of course. Who else could I be talking about? He is always getting into trouble. Every time I turn around, I'm getting a phone call from the school, church, or neighbors. The boy never settles down. I tell you, he's a bad seed. I shouldn't have had him." She shook her head as she recalled old memories.

I never heard her speak ill, about any of us. Not even after what he did to Eddie. I actually was angry at her for a long time, because of it. I couldn't understand why she didn't get mad at him. She just lost her mind, instead. After it happened, my dad kicked Darius out of the home. He told her, he had to go, or he was leaving. They ended up sending him to juvenile facility, anyway. But it wasn't long before he went awol.

"Every thing will be okay," I said, rubbing her back. She was obviously getting distressed.

"No it won't. You know it won't. You tell me all the time, you regret giving him your name. If I knew, what was going on I could have stopped all this from happening." She cried.

"Calm down." I tried to console her, but she threw me off. She was really getting worked up.

"No. Stop it. I'm tired of hiding this. Why didn't I know what was going on. It happened to me."

She really had me confused now. What was she talking about? My grandfather couldn't have been the problem. He died shortly after Darius was born. "Earl is dead." I said, trying to help clear her thoughts."

"I'm not talking about Earl, Darius. It's Larry, I'm talking about." she said with a scowl on her face.

"Larry? What does he have to do with Darius?"

"Oh god," she wailed. "I could have stopped it. I should have known what was going on."

The nurses in the courtyard started looking our way. I gave them a look that said, I had everything under control. I wanted to know where she was going. "Go on," I said, patting her back.

"It was a day like this. The sun was shining. The birds were out. Everything looked so beautiful. Then I saw it. He was on top of my boy. The bastard! The bastard!" she screamed. "How could he do that to a little boy?" she slapped her lap in frustration. "I pulled him off, but it was too late. Darius was laying on the ground bleeding. I picked him off the ground, and wrapped him up. My baby was never the same. He died that day. I should have killed my brother."

I wrapped my arms around her. She was a complete mess, now. I said, I love you, and kissed her cheek like I did as a little boy. The staff had to intervene. She was too upset to continue the visit. It was time for her to go back to her room. I was still glad, I came to see her. Because everything about my childhood became clearer after our conversation. No wonder my dad didn't want to stay home. He was reminded about what happened to her, and Darius. Our conversation also explained why she never let anyone talk bad about Darius.

266

Even after what happened he did to Eddie. The whole town knew what he did, but the police couldn't prove it. So, she didn't want to hear a word about it. I guess she felt what happened to him was some kind of excuse for his insanity.

As far as, I was concerned. One thing had nothing to do with the other. So, he was still in my sights. I had no intentions of letting our beef go. I rubbed my hand across my scared up neck. I was still putting his ass down, regardless.

Chapter 7

Darius

The last few days were a bitch. I couldn't leave my crib without dunking and dodging like a rat caught in the Matrix. My face was plastered everywhere. The other day, I heard the state was offering a hundred grand for information leading to my arrest. A hundred grand for little old me! These pigs weren't playing out here. They wanted my ass bad.

Naturally, I was on edge. I felt like all eyes where on me, because they were. Today, I went to get some food for me, Marta, and the kids. I should have been able to send her out with a few dollars, but the bitch couldn't be trusted with fifteen cents. So I had to go out, and get the shit myself. I thought I was going to get caught today. Since, a little girl pointed me out to her mom. I was at the chink store, up the street, at the time. Minding my own business, and ordering the usual. I asked Abib, or whatever his name was, for a couple of blunt sticks. So I could roll up some cush and ice, when I got home. This little girl was tugging on her mom's leg the entire time I was standing in line. She kept asking, if I was the man on television. I'd never been happier to see a hoodrat in my life. Her mom was a racket ass bitch that wasn't paying her no mind. She actually told her to shut the fuck up. I couldn't believe it. God was showing me favor. If she was decent, my ass would be locked up right now, or wetted up with lead in my chest. I couldn't have been happier to get home.

As soon as I walked through the door, I could hear the baby crying and screaming in the back room. Where the fuck was Marta and DeMarcus? I slammed the door behind me, dropped the groceries, and stomped through the house. Something was definitely off. It was easy to survey the area, unlike at night. The utilities had to go. I couldn't afford to have noisy contractors or utility workers walking around my property. It was too big a risk. Especially with DeMarcus, and the baby living here. I had to let a lot of comforts go which was starting to wear me down. This bitch couldn't carrying her weight, which wasn't make shit any easier. I was needed to get this bitch in line. Apparently, she thought I was playing.

I walked to the back screaming their names, but no one answered. When I swung the door open, I was livid. The baby was on her stomach struggling to breath, and Marta was passed out high, with a needle in her arm. I was enraged. I picked up the syringe, and started stabbing her with it. I bet the bitch would wake up now. She screamed and cried as usual. I was done playing game with her ass.

"I'm sorry. I'm sorry." she cried. "I didn't mean

to fall asleep."

I knew her ass was sorry, now. She was rolling back and forth on the bed, sobbing. If she did what I said. There wouldn't have been any problems. What the fuck am I paying her to do? She had the best job, a smoker could ask for. All she had to do was watch the fucking kids when I was gone. And the bitch couldn't even do that, simple shit? I didn't feel an ounce of simple for her stupid ass. I had better shit to think about.

I flipped baby girl on her back, and realized DeMarcus wasn't in the room. Where the fuck was his ass at? Doubled back to the front room to get the formula I bought, and threw at Marta while she was crying on the bed.

"Feed her. And change her baby too. I have to go find DeMarcus, you dumb bitch." She nodded, and reached for my baby. I slapped the bitch like she was crazy. "Clean the fuck up first. Damn! Do I have to tell you everything. I headed out to find my son. He couldn't have gotten too far away.

I crept down west side OKC with my arms stuck in the front of my hoodie, and the hood pulled down as low as it would go. It probably wasn't necessary, because the area was filled with society's waste. There was nothing but crackheads, homeless people, and strays on the street. Anyone brave enough to walk out here alone, didn't give a fuck

270

about their life or safety, let alone who I was. It was serious out here on these streets. Still, I decided to take the extra precaution anyway.

Was that his little ass, pushing the shopping cart across the street? It was. He had on the same jacket and jeans he wore, before I left for the store. He had me fucked up, if he thought he was running shit. I jogged up behind him, and grabbed his shoulder with my good hand. He spun around, and screamed so loud, I grabbed my ears. "Get off me, motherfucker!" He yelled. "I don't know you, cuss."

This bastard wasn't my son. There were people outside, chopping it up and slinging. They looked up, and turned in my direction. I knew none of them gave a fuck about what a did, but a hundred thousand dollars was a lot of reasons to call the police.

A Fat Albert look-a-like looked directly at my arm. I tried to shoved it back in my hoodie pocket, but it was too late. "Hey, Nick. Ain't that nigga, wanted? I know I saw this fool on the news last night." He nudged the short skinny man smoking a Black & Mild standing next to him.

"You right, my nigga. That's him." He turned towards the house and yelled, "Yo, Bird. Get my cell phone. It's on the side of the bed."

I hooked around the trigger in my pants pocket.

271

The other three men in the yard flashed their steel, before I could. I decided to let it go. I couldn't win a gun fight. I was at least three against one. Instead, I spun on my heels, and took off in the opposite direction. They hoped in the car, and peeled out of the driveway. I needed to get my ass home. I was running like a new slave trying to break free. I ended up hiding in a commercial trash can, for at least thirty minutes. They weren't trying to me. The saw dollar signs on my ass.

When I got home, I stunk. Every inch of my body was soar. My blood was boiling. The voices inside my head wouldn't shut up. I was angry, and ready to kick some ass. The warehouse was spotless, and quiet for a change, but I didn't give a fuck. This bitch risked my freedom. There was no forgiving that shit. But before I dealt with her, I needed to take care of me.

"Baby you hungry?" She tiptoed in the room with the baby on her hip. "I made you a plate. Do you want it?"

Did I just hear this bitch correctly? She couldn't have said, what I thought. My calculated plan was falling apart, because she couldn't watch the kids for thirty minutes. And she asking me, if I want a fucking sandwich. I broke down the blunt with shaking hands. I needed to smoke more than ever. "Get the fuck out of my face." She ran in the room with the baby.

I hit the blunt, and choked. That shit felt so good. My blood and bones relaxed, instantly, for the first time all today. Finally, I was in the right frame of mind to make some logical decisions. My thoughts weren't jumbled, and all over the place. If I was going to stay out of jail, and get Fatima back, I had to come up with a plan B that would correct the problems Marta created. First, I needed to jot down all the mental pros and cons. Pro. Fatima wasn't fucking with my brother anymore. That much I knew from writing my peeps in jail. When I got the news, he took out Butter. I actually, swelled up with pride. I never thought Dr. Do Right could survive a stint in jail. Let alone with a hardcore nigga like Butter. I paid good money to have him turned out. Apparently, I underestimated my kinfolk. Pro number two. Baby girl was still with me. She'd be the perfect bargaining chip I'd need to bring Fatima crawling back home. I ran out of pros faster than I thought. So I decided to hit the blunt again. But at least it was a start.

"This nigga must be crazy. Pros and cons? There ain't no fucking positive side to this shit." a voice said, from across the room.

I jumped off the couch, and started swinging. "Who the fuck said that?" looked under the couch, and around the room.

"Is everything okay, baby?" Marta rushed into the room with baby girl in her arms.

273

"I admit you were right." another voice answered.

"Yeah, nigga. I told you. Pay up. This fool is going to jail." Where were the voices coming from? They didn't sound inside of my head. I thought someone caught me slipping, but I was alone.

"I ain't going no fucking where." I screamed at the top of my lungs. They were trying to trick and confuse me, but I was too smart for that. They never won before, and they weren't going to win now.

"Baby, calm down." Marta put baby girl on the opposite hip, and rubbed my back and shoulders.

"Give me my child," I snatched my daughter away from her, and she started crying. I didn't want this dumb bitch anywhere near her.

"Darius, I'll leave you alone, just give me the baby back." She actually looked sincere, but I didn't trust her. My daughter was wailing, and screaming like I was a stranger. I couldn't figure out what was wrong with her. I tried bouncing her up and down, patting her back, and rocking her back and forth, but nothing was working.

"What the fuck did you do to her? You turned her against me." I yelled, pointing at Marta. I couldn't believe this bitch. She was setting me up at home too.

274

"Fuck you nigga. She sees right through your trifling ass. That's why she's freaking out." Tasha rolled her neck, and sucked her teeth. What the fuck was she doing here? She pushed her hands against my chest.

"Get off me. Get off me." I shrieked. Still, she kept walking towards me. "Back the fuck up, Tasha." She wouldn't leave me alone. Her face was burned, and crusted just like I remembered. I didn't understand. How could she be here?

"What's the matter nigga? You can't say hi to a bitch. Where do you think your going?" she taunted.

I flipped out. Between her nagging voice, and baby girl's cries, I lost it. I kicked her in the stomach, and started stomping her. There was no way, she was taking me out. Blood sprayed me and baby girl in the face, after every blow. I couldn't stop, until she was a puddle of mush, on the floor.

Chapter 8

Marcus

Thanks to concerned citizens a missing four year old boy was discovered, earlier today. DeMarcus Stewart, the son of the Good Wife Killer's latest victim, Tasha Stewart, was found in downtown OKC. Two good Samaritans responsible for calling police are live with us now. We'll check in with Dan for the latest details.

Thanks Patrica,

I've been standing here with these two very observant and upstanding citizens, in disbelief. Please explain, how you managed to spot him on this very busy intersection beside us, during the middle of the day?

"I was just chilling wit my girl, when I saw him walking down the street by himself."

"Uh huh, this ain't no safe area for no little boy."

"Ya mean. We just glad he got somewhere safe. And didn't get hit by a car. You dig."

"Well there you have it. I don't know about you guys at home, but I'll sleep a lot better knowing he is safe, instead of on the streets. Back to you,

276

Amy."

I closed the window on my web browser. I couldn't believe the good news. My nephew was actually alive, which meant little Briana probably was too. I pulled out my phone, and dialed Officer Moore. Even though, he said, he wouldn't help me again. I knew this situation had to be an exception.

"Moore's office," the receptionist chirped through the phone.

"Hello Misses …"

"Taylor."

"Ah, Misses Taylor. What a beautiful name. This is Dr. Du Bois. I was hoping to speak to Officer Moore. Is he in?" I made sure to emphasis doctor. Hopefully, it'd be enough to push me through without any questions.

"He's not in right now." Damn. He must have told her to block me.

"Please Miss Taylor. Patch me through. It's not about me. I really need his help."

"Hold please."

Yes. I got through. Elevator music started playing. Then I heard, a clicking sound. "Officer Moore," I asked, failing to hide the excitement in my voice.

"What do you want?"

"I don't mean to bother you, but I need a favor."

"A favor. You've got to be kidding me. Have you started smoking crack in between patients. You must not remember our last conversation.

"Whoa, whoa, whoa. Here me out. Before you jump the gun. The favor isn't for me."

"Just come out with it, already. My line is blowing up."

"The little boy they found today on Prospect and 23rd street is my nephew."

"Your nephew, huh. Why am I just hearing about this? You do understand, we're in the middle of an investigation involving a serial killer, who just happens to be your brother, right?"

"Would you like me to send a screen shot of the cord wrapped around my neck?" I didn't hide the indignation in my voice. I needed his help, but I wasn't about to let him forget who knew the situation up close and personal.

Officer Moore cleared his throat. "I'll ask you again. What do you want?"

"I want to adopt him."

With laughter in his voice he said, "Well son, I can't help you with that. You're barking up the wrong tree."

"You may not be able to help me, adopt him.

But, you can put in a good word with the social worker on his case. I want to be his foster parent. Your recommendation would speed things up. He's been through enough already. It's really the only plausible option."

"Is that right?" he said, sarcastically.

The line went dead. I nervously rubbed my head, and awaited his response. I needed to make sure DeMarcus was okay. That was the least I could do, considering I was the only sane relative he had left.

"I'll see what I can do, but I'm not making any promises."

I muted the phone, and jumped up and down in excitement. "Thanks man, you won't regret putting in a good word for me, I promise."

"It ain't for you. It's for the boy." He hung up the phone, before I could thank him anyway.

Shortly after talking to him, I received a phone call from a social worker. She needed me to come down, and fill out some paperwork. It just so happened, the shelter was overcrowded, and few foster homes where available at the time. The shelter actually started accepting toddlers, and newborns which was typically against protocol, because the system was so overwhelmed. So, she was more than happy to help. DeMarcus was coming home with me. I just needed to rush downtown to pick him up.

Getting him discharged didn't take long at all. I signed on the dotty line a few times, and he was ready to go. When they brought him downstairs, I was shocked at his condition. I couldn't help staring. He looked awful. His eyes were sullen, and dark. I needed to do a double take, he looked like a little prisoner. It was obvious, he'd been through his own personal hell. He held his face like an old man, not a child. The innocence was gone from his eyes.

"He's ready to go." The old woman who brought him downstairs said, looking hardcore. She smiled, but it didn't seem genuine. I was glad, he wouldn't be spending anymore time with her. "He doesn't have any clothes or belongings to take with him. You should call his worker. Maybe, she'll be able to give you a clothing voucher. The poor child doesn't have anything. Bless 'em." She said, shaking her head.

DeMarcus held his head down, and played with his fingers. I didn't want him to feel ashamed. "That won't be necessary. We're going to buy brand new clothes, shoes, and toys just for him."

"Really," he exclaimed. His eyes lit up, and he started jumping up and down like I did, after I got the good news.

"Really," I replied. I got on his level, and stared into his eyes. He was starting to look like a little kid already. "You ready to go?" I asked, extending my hand.

He nodded, clasped mine. A few minutes later, we were driving out of the parking lot.

On the way home, I stopped and bought him a happy meal, and an Oreo McFlurry. He was so happy. He couldn't stop smiling. Then, we stopped and picked up some clothes, hygiene products, and a few toys from Kohl's which sent him sailing over the moon. When we got back into the car. He was strangely quiet. Until then, he'd been talking since we left the shelter. Concerned. I asked, "Are you okay?"

He nodded but didn't turn in my direction, or say anything.

"You know, you can tell me whatever you want. And I can't say a word, because you're my patient." I said, while paying attention to the road.

He shook his head.

Why are you shaking your head?

"You're not my doctor. Now you're my dad, right?" He asked.

"Technically no." Immediately, he shoulders slumped, and he started to look sad.

"I'm you're uncle though." He crossed his arms, and turned his knees toward the door.

"I'll still take care of you like a dad. What do you think?"

"I hate him. If his my dad, I don't want one." I was surprised he had such strong feelings about Darius. I wasn't even sure, he knew who he was.

"You don't mean that, do you?"

"Yes I do. He's mean. I wish he was dead."

"What did he do to make you so angry?" Of course, I could totally relate. But I wanted to understand where DeMarcus was coming from. They interviewed him, after he was found, but they didn't get anywhere. He said, he didn't know to every question they asked.

"He made my sisters go away. I don't know where they are," he said with tears welling in his eyes. "He took my mom away too. I hate him. I wish he was dead."

If only he knew, how much I agreed. I pressed on, for more details. "When is the last time you saw you're dad?"

"He's not my dad!" he yelled. This time tears were streaming down his face.

"I'm sorry," I said, taking my hands temporarily off the wheel. I could totally understand how he felt. I didn't even claim him, myself. "Did you see him, a long time ago?"

"No. I saw him yesterday." He sniffled, and whipped his eyes. I wasn't sure, he understood what he saying.

"How long ago was yesterday?"

"You know what yesterday is," he crossed his arms, and looked at me like I was crazy. "The other morning. You know. Before you woke up, today."

I had to give it to him. The kid was smart. He was little, but smart. He understood, exactly what I was saying, which got my wheels turning. Maybe, he could lead me to Darius. I could rescue Briana, and kill him, if I knew where they were.

"Can I ask you a question?"

"Shoot," he answered like a little man.

"If I drove around to different buildings. Could you tell me which house Darius lived in?"

"Yeah," he nodded again.

I wanted to take him driving around, right now. But it was already ten o'clock. His eyes where low and heavy. His little head kept nodding forward. Then, he'd sit up, right before falling asleep. "Do you want to go home, now? Or do you want to help me find Darius, the super villain, like a superhero? We can help save the day, and call the police, because he is one of the bad guys?" I had to lie, and make it sound exciting. I couldn't risk him forgetting where he lived. I refused to miss such a great opportunity. The news broadcast, showed where they found him. Darius couldn't live more than fifteen miles from where they interviewed the two eyewitnesses.

"I want to be a superhero!" he exclaimed.

"Good. I'll buy you another ice cream, after we find the house." I figured a little motivation couldn't hurt.

"Yay!" he cheered.

We both were excited, and fully awake. At first, I had no idea, how I was going to find Darius. I was beginning to lose faith. I never imagined, god would send me such a little helper. But I was sure glad he did.

Chapter 9

Fatima

Her lips were black, and looked like leather. I didn't want her in my room. She gave me all types of Cleo vibes from Set It Off. Actually, that was inaccurate. Even Cleo looked soft compared to her. Honestly, she was the hardest looking woman, I'd ever seen. I didn't want to judge, but I couldn't help it. Her appearance screamed cookie snatcher. I didn't know how I was going to sleep with her lying next to me in the room. As soon as she came in the room, she was mugging.

Dr. West tried to warn me. He said, it was about time I got a roommate. Since, it was the only step left, before getting discharged. Reluctantly, I agreed. He obviously wanted me to take a leap of faith. I decided to brave it, but I wasn't expecting someone like this. Maybe, he thought we'd automatically connect. Since we're both black girls. I knew some white folks thought, we all got along. If that was his assumption, he was way off track. I planned on talking to him about my new living conditions, during my next session. At first, I thought Darius was the only person I feared. But the way my mouth dried out, and my pulse started racing, I was starting to think I was fooling myself.

She started cackling, and I jumped.

"Damn you're a scary ass bitch." she said, plopping her things down on the bad.

"Excuse me?"

"Oh. I see. You're one of those siddy bitches. I should have known. You look like the type." She sat on her bed, and crossed her legs at the ankle. Apparently, I wasn't the only one, judging a book by it's cover.

"I'm not siddy." I stuttered.

"I'm not siddy," she mimicked. "Even you're voice sounds like a white girl."

"Whatever," I moved to the opposite end of the room. Picking up my book along the way. I drug my chair in front of the window, and tried to read, but my nerves wouldn't allow it.

"If it makes you feel any better. I think you're kinda cute."

My stomach twisted into a thousand knots. I knew, she was a cookie snatcher. I threw my book on the floor, and shot up. I needed to draw the line. "Look. I'm not a lesbian. Whatever, you got swimming around in your head. Ain't gonna happen."

She started slapping her leg, and laughing like I told the funniest joke, she ever heard. "If I was a cookie snatcher. You couldn't stop me anyway. I can see you shaking, and sweating from here."

I wiped my forehead with the back of my hand. Damn. I was such a coward. Of course, I was nervous. I crossed my fingers, and hoped she couldn't tell. Unfortunately, I wasn't so lucky.

"Calm down, Hilary. I won't steal your cheeks." she wiped away happy tears, and extended her hand in my direction.

I really didn't want to take it. I didn't appreciate her making me out to be an ass. But I did anyway to keep the peace. She kissed it, and I snatched it back.

"You can give it to me, though. If you want," she started laughing again.

"Uh huh, this shit isn't gonna work." I stormed towards the door. They needed to find me a new roommate.

She jumped in front of the door, and put her hands up. "Wait. Damn. I'm sorry. I was just fucking with you okay."

It appeared, she was being honest. But I didn't care. I just wanted her to get out of my way. I tried to move past her, but she pushed me back. "Bitch, are you fucking crazy?" My adrenaline was pumping now. Was she really trying to keep me in my room.

"Look. I said, I was sorry. Please don't call staff." I could see tears welling in her eyes.

The door opened, and Mr. Price entered the room. "Is everything okay, in here?" he asked, looking between us.

Her eyes plead with me. Now she was the one sweating bullets, and looking nervous. I didn't know what to say. I wasn't trying to stir up shit. I just wanted her to keep her distance. "Everything's fine," I said, looking her square in the eyes.

"Hey, we're good." she put her arm over my shoulder. Immediately, I threw it off.

"You sure, Fatima? He asked again, looking concerned.

"I'm okay," I smiled.

"Let me know, if you'll have any problems." He left the door opened, and walked out the room.

"Damn girl. You're cool people. I thought you were going to sell me out."

"Sell you out. What are you talking about. You're the one acting crazy."

"Aren't we all." She said, laughing again.

I looked at her like the fool, she was acting like. I was right about her liking girls, but this chick was a mess. Everything that came out of her mouth was a damn joking. She was really getting on my nerves. I screwed up my face, and went to sit down. She got up, like she was going to try to shut the door, again.

"What are you doing?" I asked, spinning around.

"We need some privacy?"

"No the hell we don't. If you need privacy. Go to the bathroom. Whatever you need to say, go ahead, and say it. But there's no need to close the door." I crossed my arms, and rolled my neck. She was going to fool me again.

"Man, forget it. I was going to tell you why I got in here. But you probably don't care anyway."

I really was getting antsy inside this place. After Marcus came to visit, we started talking again. My mind started wondering what it would be like to get out. Sitting by myself in silence wasn't doing it for me, anymore. I could really use a good story to break up the boredom. "You can close the door." I sat on the side of my bed that was facing hers.

"Cool." she shut the door, and returned to her bed. "Damn this is awkward."

"You got your way. Now you don't want to tell me why you're in here." I asked, annoyed.

"Nah, that's not it. I really didn't want anybody to know. It's not the easiest thing to talk about." Her demeanor changed. She looked shy, and uncomfortable. I'm sure that wasn't normal for her, considering how loud, and rowdy she was acting before.

"Then, why the hell did you bring it up?" This woman was really starting to get on my nerves. Hell, maybe I didn't want to hear a good story after all. I really wasn't trying to pull teeth. Suddenly, I realized I didn't even know her name. And she didn't know mine, either. "Why don't we start with basic introductions. "Hi. My name is Fatima," I stretched out my arm. "What is your name?"

"I knew you were fancy." She sucked her teeth, and shook my hand. "Hi Fatima. I'm Donn." She said, smiling.

I wasn't surprised by her name, at all. She looked like a Donn. Not the type you'd find beautifully rising over the clouds, but the one you'd find on the corner selling rock. I could only imagine what she did to get in here.

"Now that we got that out of the way, tell me why you're in here?"

She fidgeted with her clothes, and rolled her neck. She sure was acting dramatic. "I killed my baby daddy." She said it so fast, I wasn't sure I heard her right.

"What did you say?"

"Damn girl, keep up. I said, I killed my son's father." This time she stretched it out, like I was

290

slow.

I got up, and started pacing the floor. She was worse than I thought. Now, I really didn't want to share a room with her. "Oh." I said, trying to hide my judgment. The last thing, I wanted to do was piss her off.

"So now you're going to start acting funny."

"Uh huh," I lied. "What makes you say that?"

"You're pacing back and forth like a rat, trapped in a corner."

"Did you just call me a rat?"

"Don't change the subject. Admit it. You look at me differently now."

I put my hands on my hips, and stared her down. I didn't think much of her to begin with. "Tell me why you do it. Make me understand. How can you hurt another human being. Especially, someone you loved."

"Shit. Your ass is too damn naive. I wish my life was as simple, and good, as yours." she said, rolling her eyes at me.

I grunted, and looked away. She could tell her business, but I wasn't sharing shit with her. "It's not my place to judge anyway. That's between you and god. He'll have the final say."

"For someone who's not judging me. You sure

291

sound like it. Why you got bring god into it, and shit. I bet you don't even have no kids."

Her words hurt. Lately, I'd been thinking about Briana everyday. At first, the psychotropics and my fierce denial tricked me into believing I was ever pregnant. But after, Marcus came, and we started talking again. I couldn't get her out of my head. I started thinking maybe, she was still alive.

"You do have a child." She said, reading my thoughts. "You look good girl, you can't even tell." I appreciated the compliment, but not the look. She was staring me down like a box of milk chocolate. Her eyes sent shivers down my spine.

"Yes. I have a daughter. Her name is Briana." I was surprised, she didn't hear about me on the news. "Here's a picture of my son," she pulled out the photo, beaming with pride. He really was a cute little boy.

"He's very handsome." I said, smiling.

"Thank you. Can I see a picture of your daughter," she asked, expecting me to reach in my pocket.

"I don't have one."

"Yeah right. I see how you is."

"For real. I've never seen her before."

"You've never seen your own child. What kind

of mother are you? You had me fooled. I thought you were one of those church types." Her eyes told me, she couldn't believe what I said. "I could never give up my child," she continued. "I'm in here, because they let me out early for attempted murder. I say I killed him, because he might as well be dead. I got that motherfucker good when he was sleeping. He's in the hospital sucking on a tube. I heard his mother is trying to decide, whether or not to pull the plug." Her face lit up like a Christmas tree. There was no denying she was proud of what she did.

"Why are you here, instead of the prison. Some people get life for less."

"Oh my case was exponential." She said, misspeaking. I'm sure exceptional, was what she meant. "I came off from work, after speeding two hours on the bus. The motherfucker forgot to pick me up from my job. When I came home, I didn't see my son anywhere. The house was quiet, and spotless. I was actually grateful, he did something while I was at work for a change. When walked into the bedroom. I found him on top of my son. He jumped out of bed, and tried to sooth me. My mind was reeling. I didn't know what to do. For the rest of the night. It was like I was in a different world. That night, we all went to bed like nothing happened. Except, I couldn't sleep. I walked down the hall, and peeked in my son's bedroom. To my surprise, he was asleep. In that moment, it hit me. It wasn't the first time, that happened. All those times, I was at working pulling doubles, he was chilling at home, raping my son. I walked to the kitchen in my night gown. I did my best to stab him into tiny pieces. Then, I picked up the phone, and called my sister. After, I told her what happened. She called the police, and picked up my son. The rest is history."

It may sound crazy, but I was proud of her. There wasn't any shame or hesitation in her voice. Her fierce protection, and love for her son, told me what I needed to do. I had to get out of here.

Chapter 10

Fatima

I smiled, and took in the view. Finally, I was getting my mojo back. I placed my shopping bags on the hotel floor, before climbing onto the kind sized bed with my box of treasures. During my stay at Saint Mary's Behavioral Ward, I received hundreds of letters from people reaching out to support me. One of the only positive things about being attacked was I learned how supportive complete strangers could be. I was amazed at their generosity. If it wasn't for all their donations, I wouldn't have been able to afford this room. In total, I received twenty three thousand dollars to get on my feet. Thanks to a fund drive ran by a local church and family owned bank. A bag of thank you cards sat on the floor for every person who wrote me while I was too sick to take care of myself. I couldn't appreciate them before, because I was too hurt and damaged. Today, I was proud to say I was ready to face my past. The next thing on the agenda was apartment shopping.

Most of the letters I read said the same thing. They prayed for me, wished me well, and encouraged me to have faith in finding my daughter. The last bit was already true. After meeting Donn, I realized I couldn't give up on myself, because I would be giving up on her, if she was still out there. Initially, it was easy for me to accept she was dead. It eliminated the possibility of getting hurt again. For the same reason, I planned on keeping Marcus at a distance, but now I completely changed my mind. If our daughter was out there. She needed us, and I had every intention to be there. In fact, I'd been trying to get in contact with him for the last few days, but he wasn't answering his phone.

The next envelope, I planned to open, read from Dimples. Immediately I started to shake. Swallowing down the lump in my throat, I prayed out aloud, "God please don't let it be him." I flipped the envelope over, and opened it. I was shocked to find there wasn't a letter inside. Instead, I found the backside of a photograph.

Hey, Fatty

It's me. You're love, and future husband. I thought you'd like to see, how our baby girl has grown.

I love you,

Dimples

P.S.

Don't be stupid. She wants to meet her mommy. It's been too long. If you give me any reason to think you're trying something slick, unfortunately, you two will never meet.

See you soon.

Tears covered my cheeks, and bumps ran down the length of my body. There was an address listed at the bottom. There was also an offer expiration date at the top right hand corner. His deadline was tonight. "Thank you god," I cried aloud. Even though, she was with the devil. My baby was still alive. I quickly flipped it over the pictured. Instinctively, I gasped, and dropped it on the floor like it was on fire. My baby girl was drenched in so much blood, I couldn't see her features. What the hell was he putting my her through? It looked like she was screaming her head off. I couldn't tell if it was hers or another person's blood. I had to get to her, asap.

My ring tone went off beside me, in the bed. I glanced over, and saw it was Marcus calling. I was too messed up to speak to anyone. I sent the call straight to voice mail. I had to clear my head. I prayed, god answered me quickly. I needed guidance, and solutions to get my Briana back. Involving police wasn't an option. And staying away wasn't either. I was going to be there, no matter the danger to myself. My tears where full of joy, excitement, and pain. I just wrapped my mind around being with Marcus again. Unfortunately, our rekindled relationship would have to wait.

I stepped outside the yellow cab with a set of shopping bags full of baby items. I set them on the sidewalk, and double checked the address on the back of her picture. In disbelief, I realized this slum was it. I grunted in disgust, and waved off the taxi. Doubtful thoughts rushed into my mind. I should have called the police, my subconscious screamed in the back of my head. What if it was a trick, and she was already dead? I shoved the thoughts away, and picked up my bags. I already lost her once, I wasn't going to risk losing her again. Standing on the sidewalk, I knew I made the right decision, the doubt only set in for a second. As if living on the west side wasn't bad enough, he had my baby sleeping in an abandoned warehouse. Getting her couldn't wait for police, or anyone else. She needed me days, weeks, even months ago. I felt shame for not getting it together fast. Strolling up to the building, I noticed it was blacked out, and crowded with so much trash, I couldn't tell if Darius was home. The seedy neighborhood made me feel apprehensive enough. The lack of streetlights, opened businesses, or signs of activity only made me more nervous. Still, I approached the front door.

Before I could reached it, a man walked up

behind me, "Hey shorty. Can I get some change off you."

I clutched my shopping bags and purse. He looked to be about twenty five. Apparently, he wasn't too old or proud to beg. I ran through my options. I could give him a few dollars to make him go away. Money really wouldn't matter anyway, if I had to live with Darius. Or I could tell him to get lost, and take my chances.

"Get the fuck out of here," I jumped back, and looked behind me. The voice I never wanted to hear again sent shivers down my spine. Darius held Briana in his hand-less arm. He pointed and cocked a gun at the stranger.

"I'm cool brother. I don't want no trouble." He put his hands up, and backed away.

Briana started to cry, and everything disappeared around me. I ran, and snatched my baby from him. She was so beautiful. She looked like a little me. I gave her my finger, and she quickly grasped it. "Hey pretty mama," I said, kissing every part of her body. I couldn't see through my tears of joy. That moment was everything to me. I waited so long to see her little face, I couldn't stop crying and singing her praises. Darius was a forethought as I strolled up to the front door. I was completely lost in the moment.

"You look good, Fatty." He said, bringing the

bags inside.

Even in the night's sky, I could see he looked much worse than I remembered. He wasn't the strong tower, I met years ago. He's clothes weren't clean, and crisp. His Cesar cut was missing. It looked like he hadn't cut his hair in months. The stink coming off him was almost too much to bare. But, my love for Briana was strong enough to endure his presence. To my surprise, I wasn't possessed with fear. For almost a year, I created every worse case scenario in my mind. I was convinced, I would fall apart, if I ever came across him again. Amazingly, fear didn't overtake me. I wasn't shaking with fear, but I was hot with anger. The worst was behind me, he had no power left. I was willing to anything to set things right.

Sitting on the couch in front of the kerosene heater and lamp, I scanned the coffee table in front of me. He was keeping track of every story with my name, or face on it. I felt a cold rush over me, but it wasn't from the cold draft inside. Darius was finally playing his last card. So far, the deck was completely stacked against me. I needed a distraction. The lack of electricity was going to make it difficult to catch him off guard. There was nothing in the room to steal his attention from me. Still, I was going to figure something out, because me and Briana weren't separating ever again.

Darius placed the items I bought onto a shelf

standing against the wall. I watched him balance foil on his wrist from a cross the room. He dropped a rock on top with his good hand, and fired up. He was definitely dedicated to the cause. He eyes rolled into the back of his head as he inhaled.

"Ooh wee, that's that good shit right there," He rolled his neck, and joined me on the couch. "Fatima, why don't you get a little taste? I promise you'll like it." He said, nudging the drugs my way.

I put Briana on the couch beside him, and started changing her diaper. "Thank you, baby. I'll have to try some later. Briana needs a diaper change, and looks really hungry. Besides, I want to spend as much time with her as I can. We've been apart for so long." He looked at me sideways like there was a devil and angle on each shoulder. God only knows what was going on inside his head.

"You've missed her, but have you missed me?" He asked with wide eyes. I knew telling the truth wasn't an option. I had to buy time.

"What do you think?" As much as it pained me, I pecked his dry lips. My stomach curdled thinking about all the possible things he pressed against them. They weren't sweet and supple like they used to be years ago, before lost his mind. Instead they were dry, rough, and worn like him.

He moaned happily, and took another hit. A small peck on the lips wasn't going to keep him satisfied for long. I had to act fast. I knew, Darius didn't debate or argue. My mind drifted to the night, I lost my best friend, Tasha. For some crazy reason, he treated me different than his other victims. If I was anyone else, I'm sure he would have killed me by now.

"Damn girl. I'm so happy you're home. I was beginning to think I'd never get my family back, again." He broke my thoughts as I finished, changing Briana's diaper. He yanked me to the side, and pulled me in between his legs. Briana was cooing, beside him on the couch. I made eye contact with her to avoid staring into his eyes.

"Look at me." He grabbed my chin, and said, "I love you." His eyes board through me. He was obviously looking for signs of deceit.

"I love you, too." I smiled weakly, and prayed my act was convincing.

He held me tight, breathed in my hair, and said, "Fatty, I can't wait to taste your sweetness. It's been so long. You don't know, how long I've been waiting for us to be together, again."

Thank god, he believed me. He released his grip, leaned back, and started tugging at the front of his pants. I knew, exactly what he wanted me to do. Images flashed through my mind of past abuses. The thought of him being inside me, shocked my system.

He placed my hand on the bulge in front of his pants.

Licking my lips, I mocked desire, and unbuttoned his pants. He rubbed his chest, and stared me down in anticipation. I have to do this. I have to do this. I might as well get it over with now. He stood up, and I sat on my knees. Looking up at him, I slowly unzipped his pants.

"Open your mouth," he said pulling out his monster.

The thought made me gag, but I couldn't show it. I obeyed, and pulled him to me.

The sound of tires rolling, came from outside. "Damn. Who the fuck is that?" he said, pulling up his pants, and scurrying across the floor. "Get down," he shooed me towards the baby, then pointed towards the door in the back. I sighed, and dropped my shoulders in relief.

Chapter 11

Marcus

Finally. The day of reckoning was here. DeMarcus was an awesome sidekick. He pointed out the abandoned auto shop with ease, a few days ago. I paid a local freshman up the street to watch him while I did what I needed to do. At first, I thought about calling Officer Moore. The publicity I received involving Darius, and his attics knocked several zeros off my bank account. I really didn't want to lose anymore. Besides, he helped me so much in the past, I almost picked up the phone. I also thought about turning around, because I didn't want to risk my practice and reputation. I worked so hard for both. But then I came to my senses. Darius was a big fish, I deserved to catch. On second thought, he was a piranha that deserved to die for almost taking my life, stealing my child, and destroying the woman I loved, and our relationship. I rubbed my neck, as an unfriendly reminded of what I needed to do.

I rolled into the back of the warehouse parking lot with my lights, and engine shut off. I peered through my tinted glass windows, and noticed flickers of light beaming through the warehouse. He was home. I quickly tucked the handgun sitting on the passengers seat in the back of my pants. Before, leaving the house I made sure to strap a holster around my waist. I carried another gun on my hip as backup. Getting out of the car quietly, I patted my hip down confirming my backup piece was snugly at my side. Then, I reached for the nine inch blade strapped to my ankle. I wasn't going to underestimate him by going into battle unprepared.

I grabbed the 9mm from my side pocket, and lurked up to the building. The parking lot was wide, and empty. The only thing breaking the silence was the sound of gravel shifting underneath my steel-toed boots. I switched off the safety, and peeked into the window. I could see candles, and a kerosene lamp from the window. I couldn't see much else, the room looked empty besides a beat up looking couch sitting in the middle of the floor. I slide to the side, and slowly reached for the door.

"You make it so easy." Darius said, with laughter in his voice. He shoved me against the door, and started jumping around the empty parking lot like we're two little kids playing freeze tag.

"You think this is a fucking game." I said, seething with anger. He was jumping around like a fool.

"Life's a game, my nigga. You're just too stupid to realize it. Maybe that's why you stay losing." I could see he was enjoying egging me on. "If you

305

took the time to learn the rules, maybe she'd be with you, instead of me." He said, wearing a mischievous grin. He threw his hands up, and started laughing.

What the hell was he talking about? I knew he couldn't be talking about Fatima. My finger clung to the trigger in my hand.

"Yeah, nigga. It's exactly what you think. My woman came to her senses, and chose the better man. She was actually preparing to suck my dick, before you rudely interrupted."

I fired in his direction. I didn't want to believe what he said. Me and Fatima were just starting to get back on track. He slide across the parking lot, and he ran by the side of the building with a gun in his hand. I pivoted, ran, and crouched behind my car. We were both out of sight from each other. "I don't believe you. Fatima wouldn't do that. She always was too good for you."

"Yeah, keep telling yourself that," he jeered. "Just remember, she never left me. I gave her to you."

"You never gave her to me. She made a decision. She couldn't handle living with your crazy ass." I said, peeking my head over the hood of the car. He fired. I jumped back, and fell on my butt. I scurried to my feet, and heard him laughing. He wasn't taking me seriously.

"That's your other problem. You're a bitch. I hate to tell you that, but it's true. Women don't want a paper tissue nigga. Why do you think they stay choosing men like me over you?" He paused for dramatic effect. I wasn't going to respond. I didn't show up to have meaningless conversation. "Fatima came back, because she respects me. She may not like my methods, but it makes her enjoy the dick even more when I'm plunging deep inside, because she has something strong to hold on to. Meanwhile, a bitch like you is at home with tears on your pillow. You're out of your league, my nigga. Throw in the towel. I really don't want to hurt you. Already had to kill one brother."

A sharp pain pierced through my back. I dropped my gun, and reached for my side. Darius picked up the gun I dropped, and stood over me.

"I told you. Go home. You're out of your league."

"Why are you doing this?" I asked, gripping the deep wound on the back of my hip. It felt like a six inch blade went through me. He came out of no where.

"Don't play innocent now. You did this. You should've let Fatima go."

"Why do you keep bringing her up. This isn't about Fatima. You need to stop. You can't keep taking people out. You've been doing the same shit,

307

since we were kids." It was true. Fatima, and the baby were my main motivation. But I also had other people like DeMarcus to think about.

"And you think a bitch like you, is going to stop me?" He gave me a pitiful smile, and circled around me. I hated how much he was enjoying seeing my down.

"If you're gonna kill me. Do it. Why keep fucking around?"

"Oh. I'm gonna kill you. That much, you don't have to worry about. I just want to stretch it out. You're brother. I want to make this moment special." He grinned.

He threw both guns across the parking lot, and started stomping me. I covered my head, and managed to kneel while taking the body shots. I wasn't going to back down, or going out without a fight. I came way to far, already. I pulled the gun out of the back of my jeans, and fired. Darius grabbed for his ankle with his missing hand. He started hobbling away.

BANG! BANG! BANG!

I kept firing, and missing. My clip was empty. I so threw the gun to the side.

"I underestimated you again." He said, laughing out of breath. "Just like I did with Butter."

Instantly, my heart started thumping harder

against my chest. There was no way he could have known what happened. "I didn't come here to talk. So shut the hell up. I have no idea what you're talking about."

"Oh, don't lie about it. You should be proud. My ears told me exactly what happened. From what I understand, he had you bent on your knees. Just moments before he put his dick in your mouth, you got the bright idea to stab him."

He waited for a response, but I didn't give him one. He could think whatever he wanted.

"You know I sent him to you, right?"

"Shut the fuck up, Darius." What was he talking about? How could he access, Butter from outside without getting caught.

"You remember my man, Eddie don't you? Well, he owed me a little favor. When I heard you got locked down. I had him place the order with Butter. He was supposed to make you his bitch."

I wish I was surprised, he could stoop so low. But nothing he did could ever shock me. My blood was still boiling, though. I regularly thought about that day. He was going to pay for what he did. "I don't believe, you were trying to hurt me, Darius. In fact. I think you wanted me to know how good you felt when Uncle Larry was plunging inside you."

He screamed. I heard him running my way,

before I saw him. "Fuck you! Fuck you!" he yelled, throwing heavy blows all over my body. "She told you. I can't believe, she told you," he cried.

I was so weak and dizzy, I could hardly move. Darius rolled beside me onto the ground. Tears were streaming down his face. He was wailing, and sobbing out of control. In all the years of my life, I never saw him cry. I'd be lying, if I said, I wasn't hurting for him. Even though, I hated him more than any person in the world. I felt bad, he went through that shit. I kept my eyes closed, and slowly reached for the knife strapped to my ankle. I got it. In one swift move, I rolled on my side, and stabbed him in the neck.

He screamed out in pain. I got on my knees, hooked my arm under his, and raised him by the wound in his neck. He cries got even louder, but it didn't stop me. I was going to put him out of his misery. I slit his throat from ear to ear. I sick joy enveloped me. I finally won. Darius rolled on his back, grabbing his throat. His eyes were wide in shock. Exhausted, I fell against the back of the car, and pulled out my cell phone. I took a few moments to catch my breath. Then, I stood up, and called Officer Moore. I had some good news, I wanted to share with him.

"Hello," he croaked, sounding asleep.

"It's Marcus."

He grumbled into the phone. I couldn't help laughing.

"What do you want? It's 3 o'clock in the morning."

Fatima stood in the door with our daughter strapped to her hip, I mumbled, "I'll call you later," and hung up the phone.

"Oh my god," she gasped, and wrapped her arms tightly around my back. I flinched, then she loosened her grip. "I'm sorry, baby."

"Don't worry about it." We walked slowly inside. She sat on the couch while I took everything in. Finally, life was going to be good again.

Fatima screamed. And I turned around. Darius was standing at the door with a gun in his hands. He pulled the trigger, but the gun jammed.

"Duck," Fatima screamed. She threw the kerosene heater over my head. It exploded in front of me, and caught him on fire. I fell onto my back. She pulled me away. Darius was howling in the flames. We both watched silently, until he died. My phone started ringing, again. Fatima answered on speaker phone.

"Have you lost you're rabid ass mind? Don't you ever call my phone this early in the morning." Officer Moore yelled. He was pissed.

We both started laughing which only enraged

him more. Life was definitely going to be good, again.